The Curious Mysterious Happenings of
Valentino and the MYSTC Lions

Book 1 written by J. J. Kat

$18.99

ISBN 978-0-578-63202-5

9 780578 632025

51899>

For Mima's Angels

Ella Lauren, whose soul touches mine.
Cameron James, a young man with a big heart.

To Ella and Cameron

"Follow your dreams no matter how
long it takes or how old you are.
Believe in yourself."

Who's Who at Villa Zoo

MAX
Leader of the MYSTC
Lions; smart, skilled thief.

SCOOTER
Has polydactyl paws, can
turn on faucets & open
windows. One tough cat.

VALENTINO
Reluctantly brave; spouts
Spanish when he's in trouble.

BULL
Brainwashed, misguided
Mastiff. Neighbor to Villa Zoo.

TINY
Tough kitty, a survivor;
can't meow but squeaks!
Loves ladybugs & eats paper.

CHAI
Skittish, screeching
diaper-wearing Calico Diva.
Loves Yoshi & her pearls.

YOSHI
Brave, kind-hearted; loves to sit-up
& is a contortionist; protects Chai.

Mima's Family

MIMA
Family Matriarch, astute &
alert to animal shenanigans.

William Wiggins Miller
"WIGS"
Good soccer player.
Loves his cellphone &
video games equally.

Benji Lauren Miller
"BEAN"
Big sister to Wigs.
Protects the animals.
Sings like an angel.

MORGAN
Mom & proud owner
of Villa Zoo Estate.

AUNT JILLIAN
Moved back to Villa Zoo
to be closer to her family.

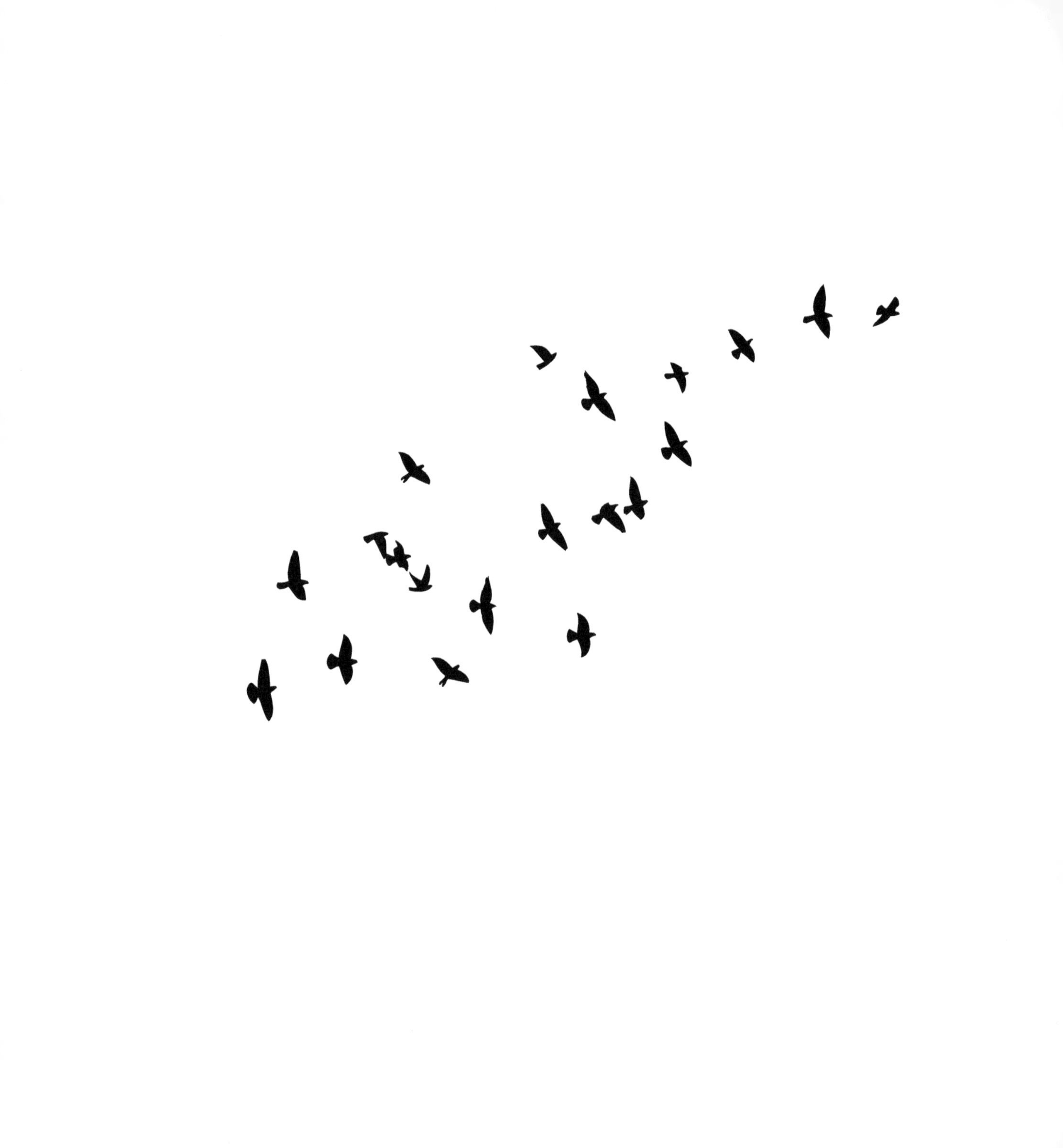

Chapter One

Like thousands of little birds fluttering in motionless flight, the trembling leaves of the quaking Aspen trees bring peace and tranquility to their universe. The slender, white branches sway to the whims of the breeze.

BUT NOT TODAY...The trembling leaves bring screams and chilling sounds of fear as the foothills erupt in danger and creepy, frightening noises.

Shadowed by a grove of Aspen trees and nestled in a meadow...surrounded by the peaceful woodlands at the base of the Rocky Mountains, Villa Zoo stands proud...mysterious. Its beauty and serenity disguise the magic that happens within its walls. *But today, outside it's walls, a battle wages between innocence and evil.*

Villa Zoo is home to Mima and her family. A mother, a grandmother, a storyteller and animal lover, Mima is a wise woman whose age contradicts her youthful energy and optimism.

While her family is packing the SUV for a trip to Denver to play in a soccer tournament, Mima has decided to take advantage of the early morning and enjoy the quiet of the outdoors behind Villa Zoo. As she sipped from a cup of coffee, a gentle breeze caressed her face and tousled her hair. She reflected on the strong hint of the hot weather to come.

SUDDENLY, the breeze turned fierce and she felt a violent tug on her coffee cup...spilling the contents. As Mima's hair swirled around her face and her dress fluttered around her, she heard the wind whisper DANGER.

Then the whirlwind stopped. The calm breeze returned. Shaking, Mima started to go back into Villa Zoo to check on her family when she saw her grandchildren coming out to visit her...unaware of the storm that had destroyed the tranquility of Mima's morning.

Her grandson Wigs and her granddaughter Bean joined her. "Mima," asked Bean. "Do you feel the magnetic energy in our home? There's a power that seduces our pets."

Regaining her balance, Mima smiled and said to Bean, "You're asking a pensive question, Bean. I think you are very perceptive. You're right, of course...our Cat Clan captivates our imagination."

"I'm wondering the same thing, Mima," said Wigs. "We've been talking and think there is something going on here that can't be explained. Mom and Aunt Jillian are clueless of the odd weirdness going on at Villa Zoo."

"I'm so proud of both of you. I'm excited to share the adventures of our animals with my foxy grandchildren," said Mima.

Mima continued. "Grownups see animals in a different way than children do. To adults like your mom and your aunt, an animal is a pet...a joy to live with and an important part of the family."

"Children see beyond. You two are aware of the aura of mystery inside Villa Zoo," Mima continued.

"I've noticed some unexplained noises and changes in the house," said Mima. "A window that is open when I know I closed it. Water running in the kitchen and a thud followed by a hasty scurry when I walk into the room. I've noticed messes when I had just cleaned the very spot earlier."

Mima went on. "I've noticed an unlocked door when I know I had locked it earlier. I hear whispering at night when I know my grandchildren are sleeping and the house should be quiet."

"The Cat Clan is anything but normal," Mima cautioned. And so is this day, she thought... remembering the wind and the whisper of danger.

Within the walls of Villa Zoo live Valentino, a tiny dog, and the Cat Clan...Max, Yoshi, Scooter, Tiny and Chai. They're **Unique**...**Fun**...**Naughty**...**Nosy**...**Mysterious**.

Valentino, a charming, white-furred chihuahua, likes to be carried. If he has to take a walk, Morgan ends up carrying him home. One day he was sure someone laughed at him so now he refuses to take the walk.

Caring for these unusual animals are Mima and her widowed daughter, Morgan Scott Miller, mom to Mima's fourteen-year-old granddaughter, Bean, and her 10-year-old grandson, Wigs.

Mima's other daughter, Aunt Jillian, recently moved into Villa Zoo. She left Florida to return to her native Colorado and her family.

"Villa Zoo is the home of the MYSTC Lions," Mima thought. But she wisely kept that thought to herself.

$$\gtrless\bullet\lessgtr$$

Scooter was on Max's shoulders. They had just come in from checking on some alarming noises outside and Scooter was closing the window.

"Max!" Scooter whispered. "You are leaning too far back and I can't latch this window."

Max adjusted. He leaned too far forward and Scooter fell into the window. He smashed his nose and left kiss marks...a dead give-away they were doing something they shouldn't do.

Max suddenly dropped to all fours. Scooter was left to fall to the floor. He flattened like a pancake.

"Hey, putz, are you okay?" asked Max as he bent over to help Scooter up.

"I don't need your lame help. I fell by myself...I can get up by myself," said Scooter as he rubbed his nose and his chin. "You're always doing that."

"Doing what?" asked Max.

"Dropping down when I'm on your shoulders...depending on you, I might add. You left me hanging in the air. I think you're getting easily distracted in your old-age," said Scooter.

Scooter pulled himself up and looked at Max who was sitting, watching him. Max said, "We've got some noises outside that I'm worried about. Did you see the size of those paw prints?"

Scooter continued to rub his sore nose and red chin. He said, "Yup, I saw them and they don't belong to any animal I'm familiar with."

Max, the intellect of the Cat Clan, removed his glasses. "I think we have a Curious Mysterious

Happening," he said...as he readjusted the glasses over his long, white fur.

Excitement for adventure was visible in the twinkle of his blue eyes. Max was the biggest, most intuitive and the bossiest of the Cat Clan. Because of his remarkable confidence, he thought glasses gave him an air of authority.

He wore an old pair of glasses he found one night when the cats were chasing one another in the storage room, causing an avalanche of boxes. In one of the boxes, he found the glasses. Max put them on his furry face...over his penetrating blue eyes...and hasn't taken them off since that day—except to clean them or hide them from Morgan and Aunt Jillian.

"You are so right," Scooter shuddered, thinking of the noises and the paw prints. "We are going to have to tell the others. When the humans leave, we'll investigate this." Scooter thought of the unexplained roars and the sorrowful wailing. His eyes began to illuminate with the thrill of doing battle!

≳•≲

Outside, a flurry of activity was happening at Villa Zoo. Morgan, Bean and Wigs were packing the SUV for a trip to Denver to play in a soccer tournament. Mima knew it would be late tonight before they returned home.

"Mom," Bean said as she came out of the house still dressed in her nightclothes. "Here's the empty bag you wanted." She handed over a large pink tote along with a purple and teal soccer ball.

"Thanks honey," said Morgan as she packed the loose items into the tote. "Did you remember to pack a change of clothing? And your large water bottle?"

"I left everything on my bed. I'll run back and...," said Bean as she entered their home, her final words disappearing with her.

"When you come back, bring the snacks I packed for the two of you," Morgan called. "They're in the blue refrigerated tote on the chair by the front door."

Morgan returned to packing the car. She heard grunting noises coming from the doorway. She looked up to see her blond-haired son, Wigs, come out of the house. His face, hands and feet were visible. The rest of him was hidden behind a pile of stuff.

Wigs still wore his pajamas. He held a change of clothing, soccer shoes with socks falling out, shin guards and a large red water bottle. He was playing a game on his phone as he walked. The change of clothing and the water bottle had slipped from his grip and were falling to the ground.

Fearing the inevitable, Morgan said, "Wigs, you're not paying attention. Any moment now, you'll trip over your clothes and come skidding down the driveway. Stop where you are."

With amazing obedience, Wigs stopped.

Morgan reached him and took the phone from his grip. "Thank you," she said. "I'm turning off your phone for the day."

"But Mom, I need my phone. I'll be bored on the looong car ride to Denver if I don't have it," whined Wigs.

"You can read a book or play a game with your sister on the way there. I'll return the phone to you for the drive back tonight," said his wise mother.

She removed the stuff from Wigs' arms. Then she picked up the items on the driveway and returned to the car to finish packing. A disappointed Wigs was left on the driveway...trying to figure out life without his phone.

Bean ran out of the house with the snacks, a change of clothing, her soccer ball, and her water bottle. She carried a large piece of paper. "Mom, I think you forgot the soccer team schedule."

As the words left her mouth, a strong breeze swooped in and grabbed the paper from her hand.

Startled, Bean looked down at her empty hand. "Mom, I'm sorry. The wind came up so fast. I couldn't hold onto it." She watched helplessly as the piece of paper flew away.

Driven by the determined breeze, the paper soared through the air. It suddenly dropped to the street and rolled to a stop.

"I'll get it, Mom," Wigs said as he ran toward the runaway paper. His strong soccer legs carried him effortlessly down the street.

Before Wigs could reach the spot where the paper had settled, the fickle wind swooped it up and whisked it out of his reach. The family watched helplessly. Without warning, the intense force flew the paper over their home and out of sight.

Morgan saw her children's frustration. "That's okay, Wigs. Come back and help me finish packing. We don't have time to hunt it down. And don't worry, Bean," said Morgan kindly. "I'm sure the Wilsons have a copy."

Wigs returned to the car. Bean helped her mother while Wigs put another load into the SUV.

The paper continued its flight over the house. It reached a spot high over the woodlands behind Villa Zoo. As quickly as the wind had picked up the paper and sailed it over the house, it released its grip.

Down to the ground it circled...until it landed on an enormously large black animal.

"Aargh," came the frightening sound from the mouth of the startled beast. Spooked by the unexpected invasion, the sleek animal bared its sharp teeth, letting a second low growl escape from its mouth. "Aargh, aargh."

The drooling, angry animal lifted its head upward. "Aargh, aargh," it said, scaring birds from the safety of their perches high in the trees.

"Eek, eek, eek," squeaked the targets of the beast...two tiny, frightened animals. Scared, with nowhere to hide, they ran around in circles trying to get away from the ear-piercing shrieks.

The black beast turned to face his targets. "Aargh, aargh," he said as he slowly advanced towards the two trembling creatures. Turning to run away from the giant stalking animal, they ran into some trees near a grouping of rocks at the base of the Rocky Mountains.

Desperate to get farther away from the roaring black beast with large paws and long, sharp nails, the animals burrowed deep under the rocks. Numbed by fear, and propelled by a need to survive, they didn't see the second pair of dark, piercing eyes watch them as they scurried deeper into the rocks.

While two vicious animals with a strong craving to grab and eat the innocent creatures who roamed the woodlands...while two lost and frightened mountain creatures were fearing for their lives behind Villa Zoo... *Mima walked out of the house carrying pillows and blankets for the car.*

Worried about the danger that threatened her home and the animals who lived within its walls, she hurriedly put the bedding into the back end of the SUV.

She told Morgan she would be gone until late the next night. "I'm meeting friends in Denver. We have dinner plans, so I'll stay overnight and start back early tomorrow evening," she said as she hugged her family and wished them a fun day.

Grabbing her overnight bag and purse, Mima got into her car. She backed the car into the street and drove away in the early morning of this new day. In the rear view mirror, she watched as her family and home became smaller images. "Have a safe day," she said aloud, anxiety bringing unwanted tears to her eyes.

Mima tried to put aside the jitters gnawing at her as she thought of the animals she was leaving behind. She realized this was not going to be an easy day for them. They were rascals and would not walk away from danger. She knew this with scary certainty.

As she drove down the street, she saw a tornado of dust flying into the air behind Villa Zoo. Bushes stirred, trees shook...inflamed by some frenzied movement.

Fear rushing through her veins, Mima pulled her car over to the side of the road. She parked and got out.

"Maybe I can get a sense of what is happening behind our home by watching. I hope I see something that'll tell me what's causing this turmoil," she worried. "Other than the earlier windstorm, the day is peaceful." But she couldn't forget the wind and the whispers of danger she experienced earlier behind Villa Zoo.

"There's no sign now of a weather storm heading our way. But a different storm— a more dangerous one—was coming." This she knew without a doubt. She was haunted by anxiety.

Chapter Two

Just as Mima was about to return to her car, she heard hideous growls and frightened, high-pitched cries.

"I wish this wasn't happening in the backyard of Villa Zoo. At least my family will be away," she thought, reminding herself that the animals would be home. "Maybe it's just the mountain critters playing in the forest." But she heard the growls...frightening noises. Mima turned and hurried to reach her car.

"I'll call Morgan and Jillian later," she said aloud as she opened the car door. "I want them to be aware of the dirt flying and the branches quaking in the backyard...caused, I'm convinced, by those hideous howls. Hopefully they'll be cautious when they return home tonight."

As Mima was about to get into her car, she saw the bushes convulse...pulsating from an unknown force. The movement began in slow motion. **Suddenly**...the leaves and branches burst into a fury. Several cyclones of dirt reached for the sky. A chilling madness had descended on the forest.

Mima got into her car. With fear in her eyes, she drove away. Her worry about the safety of her pets became intense.

"If Max and Scooter hear the howls and the cries, they won't be able to let it go."

Deep into a plan they were hatching, Max and Scooter paused. "Again, I heard that same growl coming from outside Villa Zoo. The one we heard earlier. It's so close to our home," said Max.

"I hear it, too," Scooter said. "It's a noise that sounds like one of Valentino's toys when he bites the squeaker. It made an eek eek sound. There was shrieking...lots of shrieking."

"There's craziness in the trees behind the house. I think something menacing has invaded the woodland. It's preying on innocent animals who live in freedom behind Villa Zoo," said Max.

Max and Scooter ran to the patio door. They saw dirt flying in the air. They saw stones rolling down the hill. Branches of the small bushes swayed wildly. Leaves on the trees rustled angrily as if a storm was bearing down on them.

Yoshi and Chai ran upstairs to where Max and Scooter were pacing. "Something is happening outside," they said with excitement...their eager words colliding.

"We searched earlier for some explanation," said Max. "Except for some large paw prints, we didn't notice anything threatening. **The crying...the howls...are intensifying**."

"I saw a black form move through the bushes!" Yoshi said as she ran into the room. "I couldn't tell what it was, but it was shadowy...slow, rigid and focused. It's large black eyes watched Villa Zoo with an intense stare," Yoshi continued.

Chai said, "I saw a black creature stalk a crying animal." Shivering...trembling with excitement, the others listened as Chai described what she saw.

"Squeak, squeak!" Tiny said as she came into the room. She leapt onto the sofa and dove for the chair. Restless excitement propelled her through the air.

"Realize my friends...the MYSTC Lions must act," said Max...as he continued to pace.

All nodded furry heads in heightened enthusiasm.

Max stopped pacing and raised his paw. "Cool the eagerness," he said.

They heard Max but their heartbeats remained elevated with excitement.

"Feline fighters," Max the orator began. "We are facing an unknown danger. We are aware that a threat of harm lies outside the walls of Villa Zoo. I am the oldest and the wisest of the Cat Clan. My approach is to remain alert until the family has left. Then and only then we'll probe...explore. The Curious Mysterious Happening in our backyard has aroused the warrior in each of you. But it's premature...relax fighters!!"

Max removed his glasses. He paused, looked at his family...then his glasses. He put them back on his face, adjusted them and said, with control, "Sleep, rest. We'll wait for our family to leave."

Disappointed, the Cat Clan settled into restless napping. Time passed. The noises outside continued. **Soon** cat snores filled the air.

"We're all eager to investigate this Curious Mysterious Happening. It's difficult for the others to relax once they know something is wrong. They're warriors. They're alert," said Max to Scooter.

He remembered Mima's earlier words...'This is a day of danger.' "How does Mima know those things?" he wondered. Max shook. Because of the anticipation of battle for sure, but, like Mima... he worried about the safety of his cat family.

Scooter was pacing back and forth near Max. He said to him, "The noises continue...I'm restless."

Sporting a crooked grin, Scooter redirected his thoughts to a delightful subject. He said, "We are all hungry and soon we'll be alone." He winked at Max.

"Glad you brought up a more delicious topic," said Max, as he eyed a soccer sock that fell out of a packed bag. He was tempted by the large red sock. "Yes, yes, yes...an easy drag of the sock to my water bowl would satisfy this nagging urge. Then I could get back to business," he said. "Hold the food thought for a moment, Scooter."

With a gleam in his eye reserved for the pleasure of fetching and pilfering, Max eagerly walked to the red soccer sock, took hold of it with his teeth and dragged it to the kitchen. He dropped it into his water bowl. With a satisfied grin, Max trotted back to Scooter. They huddled to discuss their food plans.

"We want to get our paws on the special Tuna Power Cakes. Because of this threat of serious danger, we need to eat two Tuna Power Cakes consecutively to bring on our super powers if we're going to solve this Curious Mysterious Happening."

For the next few minutes, Max and Scooter talked quietly with one another. Then they broke their huddle with a paw slap. The others lifted their sleepy heads and then, uninterested, fell back to sleep...cats being cats. But cats on high alert...ready to become the MYSTC Lions.

Their plan firmly in place, the two gatos rudos headed to the kitchen and...THE PANTRY!!

"I hope we get a chance to see Aunt Jillian before we leave," Morgan said to Bean as she put the last items into the car.

"I thought she would be home by now. She planned to be in Denver by the start of the tournament," Morgan continued.

"It would be nice to say hi to her before we leave but we'll see her in Denver," Bean said, before she ran back to the house.

She hollered to her mom, "I'm going to change my clothes. Wigs is, too. We'll be ready to leave soon, mamacita."

Morgan smiled as she thought of Bean's affectionate name for her.

The car was packed. Bean and Wigs showed up as promised with their soccer clothes on.

"I'm glad to see you're dressed and ready to leave," Morgan said. "Let's see if the Wilsons are." The Wilsons' children were playing in the same soccer tournament. The families planned to leave together.

"We have one more thing to do, Bean and Wigs. I need you to get every animal into the lower level of the house," Morgan said. "We've been outside for a good hour this morning, leaving them alone in the house and to their own mischief. We probably should have put them away before we packed the car." As she closed the car door, she remembered back to unexplained messes after they'd been left alone other days.

As Morgan was unaware of the commotion in the foothills behind Villa Zoo, she couldn't know of the danger lurking in her backyard. She couldn't know of the decision the Cat Clan made to check out the threatening noises.

It was better for her day if she remained oblivious.

"Let's go check in with the Wilsons."

As Morgan, Bean and Wigs began their walk to the Wilsons' house, Wigs realized he'd left his soccer ball inside Villa Zoo.

"I'll be over in a minute," he said. "I have to get my soccer ball."

"I thought we packed it, Wigs," said Morgan. "I'm glad you remembered it."

WHEN THE DAY BEGAN...

Before the shrieking and howling...
Before the dirt was flying in the air...
Before the trees swirled as if caught in the grip of a cyclone...

Max and Scooter devised a plan that involved their favorite treats...**TUNA POWER CAKES!!!**

A nosy Max and a naughty Scooter...both eavesdropping, of course...heard the family discuss a trip to Denver for a soccer tournament. The charming, meddlesome duo saw an opportunity to steal enough Tuna Power Cakes from the pantry to enjoy a cake every three hours during the day. Morgan gives them **ONLY ONE Tuna Power Cake** a day!!!

The favorite food of the Cat Clan, one large Tuna Power Cake for each ordinary cat (*at the time of their PLAN, they were ordinary cats*) tasted "Oh...so...yummy". *As everyday cats, they would sit at the table together as a family. They would talk about their day as each cat enjoyed one cake. Then they would clean up their mess with their tongues and take a long nap in the sunshine.*

After a satisfying nap, Scooter would probably open a window and take a walk outside while Max would find a pillow to take to his water bowl.

While Scooter was walking the foothills and Max was dragging a pillow, Yoshi would probably be chasing Chai while Chai was hoping her diaper didn't fall off. Tiny would be busy watching ladybugs.

Then they'd probably be tired so they'd take a nap again...and all would be right in their ordinary cat world.

NOW, SUDDENLY, WITH DANGER LURKING IN THE BACKYARD, Scooter and Max knew the Cat Clan had to be ready to Engage in Combat at a moment's notice. Their *"Eat a Tuna Power Cake, Relax and Nap Away the Day"* plan will have to wait for another day.

Warriors battling a Curious Mysterious Happening require incredible strength and endurance. After TRANSMYSTC MUTATION they will be strong, powerful lions. As MYSTC Lion warriors they require the power that TWO Tuna Power Cakes provide when eaten together.

As the others slept, Max and Scooter put their plan into action. When they reached the pantry door, Max stood tall and held his position firm as Scooter climbed up on Max's shoulders to build a Cat Tower. Scooter reached for the doorknob and turned it. The door creaked open.

Without warning, Scooter lost his balance and fell against the door, causing it to crash into the pantry shelves and throw their Cat Tower off balance.

"I thought we had perfected this," Max growled between his clenched teeth. As they teetered, Max grabbed Scooter's legs in an attempt to steady their Cat Tower. Still off balance, Scooter unexpectedly backflipped down Max's back and off his rump. Scooter hung upside down. Unable to hold on any longer, Max let go of Scooter's legs.

"Yikes, I'm falling," roared Scooter. He tumbled to the floor. Max fell backwards, landing on top of Scooter.

"Perfected? Apparently not well enough, bonehead," Scooter said as he pushed Max off and got up onto all four paws.

"Let's try this again," said Max. He straightened his glasses and stood upright.

Scooter stood up on his hind legs, then jumped up onto Max's shoulders.

After some swaying back and forth, they pulled themselves together to stand tall. Balanced, Max carefully shuffled the few steps across the floor to the pantry shelf.

"There they are," said Scooter, his face beaming. "A large supply of Tuna Power Cakes," he said excitedly. Four bags lay neatly on the shelf.

"It's all ours for the entire day," Max drooled. "We can't take them all or Morgan will know. I wonder who she'll blame for the missing bags."

"Hmmm...hopefully Valentino," said Scooter. "Reconsidering this, why don't we take two packages?"

Being a polydactyl cat, Scooter was born with more than the normal number of toes on his front paws. Plus, he had thumbs. His large paws gave him unusual cat talents. He could swiftly grab the bags of TPCs and hop off Max's shoulders with the cakes safely in his grasp.

"I couldn't agree more," said Max, nodding his head enthusiastically.

Trying to maintain a stable Cat Tower, Max moved closer to the shelf the Tuna Power Cakes were on. Scooter grabbed the shelf with one paw while he used the other to reach for a bag of the special cakes. As his paw touched the bag, the front door opened.

Wigs ran in through the open doorway. "I know I left my soccer ball near the pantry," Wigs muttered to himself.

Max was distracted after hearing Wigs' voice. He dropped to all fours...and forgot about Scooter.

Scooter felt Max leave him and quickly grabbed another shelf with his other paw. The bag of Tuna Power Cakes fell, hitting Max on the head. It bounced off his head and landed, opened, on the pantry floor. Scooter was left to hang from his big paws, his legs swinging in the air.

"Max," growled Scooter. "Get me down! Hurry! Hustle!"

Fiercely annoyed, Scooter wanted out of the pantry. "Don't want to get caught! Wigs is coming!"

Max shoved a thick towel under Scooter. Scooter dropped down, just missing Max and completely missing the towel.

Scooter picked himself up and rubbed his sore fanny.

Max shoved the bag of Tuna Cakes under another towel that had fallen to the floor. In a hurry, he didn't fully cover the bag of cakes but there was no time to fix it.

"Let's pretend to drink water from the bowls on the floor," Max whispered. "Are you okay, Scootzie? That was a close call."

"Yes," said Scooter. "No thanks to you, you bespeckled, jumbo scaredy-cat. Now we'll have to wait to remove the bag of Tuna Power Cakes from the pantry floor."

Scooter checked around to make sure no treats had fallen out of the bag. When he was certain they had not lost any of their precious Tuna Power Cakes, Scooter hurried to meet Max.

They hid behind the pantry door and listened to Wigs' hurried footsteps.

"Here it is," said Wigs. He picked up the ball from under the dining table, then he hurried out the front door.

The cats heard Wigs leave the house...the door slamming shut behind him. An agitated Max strolled to the water bowl near the pantry cabinet. "Guess I am a little thirsty," he said as he licked up water.

A sweating Scooter said. "That was bloody close."

It was then that Max realized he'd lost his glasses. "Scootzie, do you see my glasses? I must've lost them in all of the commotion."

Scooter looked around. "No, I don't. Wait a second...," he said as he looked up. There lay the glasses on a shelf above his head. The glasses, astride a peanut butter jar, lay just out of reach. "How did they land there?"

"That is a curious happening," Max said giggling. Scooter grimaced at his friend's rare attempt at humor.

"Ready?" Scooter asked. As Max nodded yes, Scooter jumped up onto Max's shoulders. Stretching in perfect form, he masterfully grabbed the glasses from the shelf, then hopped off Max's shoulders and down to the floor.

"Perfect execution," Max said, taking the glasses from Scooter and putting them back where they belong...above his nose and over his ears. "Thanks, grumpy chum," Max said as he secured the glasses onto his ears. "Sometimes you're a cool guy."

"We're lucky Wigs' attention was all about his soccer ball," said Scooter, poking Max in the shoulder. "And I'm always cool. You're just too arrogant to admit it."

On all fours again, the two cocky cats strutted out of the pantry.

"No one will guess we tried...and failed to execute our plan," said Max.

"A plan, doofus, that ended with us flattened on the floor," said Scooter.

"Well, at least the Tuna Power Cakes didn't get crushed by your nosedive. You landed on your fanny which would have smashed the cakes. Lucky for us you missed them. They're safe and easy to reach. I hid the bag under a towel," said Max.

"If nobody needs the towel before we get back..." Scooter grumbled, sarcasm rolling down his tongue and out his mouth.

As Max and Scooter nonchalantly made their way through the kitchen, they noticed Valentino, the spoiled chihuahua.

"He sure takes a lot of naps during the day, especially now since his old kennel has been replaced with a new and larger deluxe doghouse," Max said. "It's big enough for sleepovers."

"Except with Bull," said Scooter.

"Aha, you mention Bull. That mean dog is devoted to terrorizing us...he's probably hiding in the bushes right now...waiting for us to leave the house," Max said. "He's a gigantic dog! A terrifying... mean mastiff! Bull is an appropriate name for him...short for Bully."

They watched the small white chihuahua with the kisses collar disappear in his kennel.

"Valentino sure likes to burrow under those fluffy blankets Morgan bought for him," said Scooter. "He's in and out of that kennel and Villa Zoo all day, searching for attention or food. He plays outside with Wigs and Bean. He romps around in the clear mountain air. The Cat Clan isn't invited to play outside. He tires...comes inside and sleeps. What a life!"

"He has an easy life," sighed Max.

"What do you mean easy?" asked Scooter. "He's pampered, spoiled and cute."

"Morgan is captivated by Valentino's charm and loyalty," said Max.

"Yes, Valentino can do no wrong," harrumphed Scooter sarcastically.

"Valentino is always into mischief. He'll apologize, but only if he's in a generous mood," said Max with a laugh. "Valentino always looks guilty."

Scooter guffawed. "Valentino's a small dog to us but in his exaggerated brain, he's big, tough and beautiful...a fierce watchdog."

"He barks 'mad dog...beware!' " Scooter snickered. "Valentino thinks his job is to protect our family. I admit he does with great bravado...he takes his job seriously."

Max and Scooter both agreed they were glad Valentino was part of the family.

"He does not understand failure," said Max with a grin, "though I don't like it that he calls us dos gatos rudos in his sleep."

"He says that? What does it mean?" Scooter asked, making his way to the sink for a drink of water.

"Two rude cats," Max translated. He glared at Valentino...then turned and cantered away.

Scooter laughed, shaking his large, rotund body. He forgot about Valentino. Scooter jumped up onto the counter and over to his favorite water faucet.

Valentino heard the two alpha cats discussing him. "They're jealous of my cushy life. Morgan does seem to adore me," he thought. He grudgingly admitted to himself that Morgan and Mima and the rest of his human family love all their crazy, wonderful pets. "And, if I decide to admit it out loud, I do have interesting friends," he sighed.

When Valentino is in his spacious home, he observes and...snoops.

He's nosy and loves to get into everybody's business.

As Valentino was thinking about Max and Scooter and what they had been up to he heard a loud **THUMP** at the window in the lower level. He wasn't too quick to check out the noise though. Sometimes he's willing to let someone else be brave.

Scooter was called Moody Scootzie by Max and the others. They all agreed the big orange cat's emotions and actions often conflicted. But Max wouldn't be able to lead the MYSTC Lions without him. Max stopped to watch Scooter. With an ease Max envied, Scooter jumped up onto the kitchen counter. When he reached the sink, he turned the faucet on.

"That cat is tough, a real brawler," thought Max as he headed towards his favorite pillow. "Glad he's on my team."

Scooter really despised sharing a water bowl with the rest of the cats. He preferred the cool, fresh water from the faucet. He lowered his head to get a drink.

"Aaaa, cold water," Scooter said, testing it with a paw. Before he could take a sip, he heard a **THUMP**. He paused...listened intently. **THUMP**. He heard it a second time.

Not bothering with a drink, he turned the water off, jumped off the counter, and made his way downstairs.

Chapter Three

Valentino heard Max and Scooter sneaking around in the pantry. He knew what they were up to.

"Hmmm," Valentino said to himself. "I am more interested in pursuing an idea I have than in checking out that **THUMP**.

He just saw Scooter head downstairs. Valentino figured Scooter was checking out the **THUMP**. "Fine with me," he thought.

He heard Scooter stating his obnoxious mantra.

> *Don't mess with me.*
> *My paws are huge and flat*
> *Down you'll go with just one whack.*
> *I'll come to you when I want more*
> *Until then just watch and adore.*
> *Yes, I look cute when I'm at rest*
> *But you're sure to mistake this cat's best.*
> *My teeth are sharp*
> *My bite is quick and deep*
> *So don't come near me before I sleep.*
> *And when I'm sleeping,*
> *You're off limits in the space I'm keeping."*

Valentino trembled at Scooter's words. "Yup, I'll leave the **THUMP** to Scooter. I'll stay up here and work on my plan," thought Valentino.

His idea grew into a plan after he saw Max and Scooter leave the pantry. The *dos gatos rudos*, deep in conversation, were unaware he was watching them.

He'd ask about the **THUMP** later. Valentino preferred to wait until Max and Scooter had already figured it out.

Valentino left his doghouse. He focused on his plan...and couldn't hold back the big grin that filled his face!

Max wasn't as agile as he was when he was younger, but he was still a cat powerhouse. When he stood his full height, he dwarfed the others...except for Scooter...who wasn't as tall as Max. But Scooter had a bigger and more solid body.

Max walked toward his water bowl. He had *the* pillow, also known as Morgan's *favorite* pillow, in his mouth, ready to drop it into his water bowl for a good soaking. "I get goosebump pleasure dragging things to my water bowl and soaking them. If a blanket doesn't fit in my cat dish, I let it lay aside the bowl...only a corner of the blanket soaking in the water," he purred. The image soothed him. As he was reveling in this pleasant thought, he was abruptly interrupted by a loud **THUMP**.

His ears alert...back...he listened. He heard the **THUMP** sound again. He knew the noise was coming from the lower level. Max knew the family was outside. He hoped they had not heard the mysterious thuds.

"It seems Scooter heard the **THUMP**." Max watched as Scooter leapt from the counter...assumed warrior form...and made his way downstairs. He's uttering that annoying verse again...preparing himself for battle," Max said, rolling his eyes.

Max followed Scooter down the stairs.

Hiding behind his kennel, Valentino watched Max and Scooter head down the steps to investigate the thump sounds.

"Can it be," Valentino said, "that I'm actually alone? No one can see or hear me? Tiny, Chai and Yoshi are asleep in the back bedroom. Wigs left the house with his soccer ball. The family is outside packing for a trip. The two bossy cats are on a mission.

Yes! Yes! Yes! It's time," he barked. He fist bumped the air...grinning broadly as he set out to put his wicked plan in motion. He glanced around suspiciously with every step his little legs took.

Scooter reached the bottom of the steps before Max. He took long leaps, then bounced from the floor onto the sofa. From the sofa, he jumped to the ledge of the lower-level window of Villa Zoo.

"I'm certain this is where the noise came from," Scooter said.

Max arrived at the bottom steps in time to see Scooter charge the window.

"Scooter," shouted Max. "Stop! Don't open the window! You know there's trouble out there. Find out where those hideous noises are coming from first before you invite danger into Villa Zoo."

Scooter ignored Max's warning and used his large paw to unlatch and open the window.

Chapter Four

WHOOSH...four tiny, bloody mice pushed Scooter down, then ran over him.

Startled, Scooter rolled from the window ledge and fell to the sofa. Once upright, he leapt—no, he flew! A flying, not-so-brave cat landed at Max's feet.

"What was that?" a frazzled Scooter asked a smirking Max. "It...they...ran over me. I'm bleeding," cried Scooter. "I never saw what came through the window."

"Well, bozo warrior-hero, hero-warrior," Max said, "it seems you opened our home to intruders. **You** are not bleeding. **Our intruders are bleeding.** They ran over you with their bloody feet."

As Max and Scooter watched on in disbelief, four terrified mice jumped from the window ledge and landed on the floor. Their high-pitched cries pierced the air.

The disoriented mice scampered across the carpeted floor. Bleeding from tiny cuts on their bodies, they ran madly around the room. They ran into each other and into the furniture. They ran into the walls and into each other again.

Max was the first to find his voice. "There's so much blood... and they're so scared," he said to Scooter. "What happened to these poor creatures?"

"Not a clue...but we need to find out what has frightened them," said Scooter. "Whatever happened to them outside brought

The Curious Mysterious Happenings of Valentino and the MYSTC Lions

them a great deal of harm. We need to help them."

"They seem unusually disoriented and frightened...so much blood from little sores on their bodies," Max said. "They're young babies."

"Maybe they were separated from their mother and got hurt while they were trying to find her," Scooter wondered. "She must be worried about them."

"I'll get some wet, soapy rags and a net. Let's catch them...clean them and take care of their wounds," said Max. "I saw a basket and a soft blanket in the storage room. We can keep them safe in the blanket once we catch them."

"We're going to need everyone's help," said Scooter. "It won't be easy. They're not going to let us help them without a struggle. We are cats after all."

"I wonder where their mother is," said Max. "I hope she's still alive."

Max knew something else was wrong with the mice, but he couldn't work out what it was.

As Max expressed his concern about the mother, a giant, purposeful mouse with fire in its eyes charged through the open window. She stopped...saw the two cats and glared into Scooter's eyes.

"Must be Mamma Mouse," said a wise Scooter.

The injured babies found protection in a corner of the room. Frozen in fear...crying...they were unable to move.

When Mamma Mouse spotted her children, she jumped to the floor from the ledge and ran to comfort them. She was determined to protect her little ones from any more harm. "My poor children," she squeaked as she put her protective body around them. "You're so bloody and frightened. I won't let anything happen to you." She wiped away the blood with the moisture from their tears...she kissed their many sores.

She continued to glare at Max and Scooter as she comforted her children. With caution, she guided them to some protection behind a chair. Mamma Mouse would keep them safe until she had an escape plan.

Max and Scooter watched the scene playing out in front of them.

SUDDENLY...from the top of the stairs...a pathetic bark broke the silence.

"I'm not feeling very well," Valentino thought. Perspiration was running down his face. He had returned to his kennel. Alone, not finding the comfort he needed, he reluctantly dragged himself from his doghouse to the top of the stairs.

"Max and Scooter, **I need you**. *I need your help*," he whimpered as he continued to drag himself to the open stairway and the long, scary trip down the steps.

Something was very wrong with his wet, pain-racked body.

"I can do this," Valentino whispered as he looked down to the bottom of the steps. He hesitated before beginning his descent. As he took the next step, he lost his balance and rolled down the stairs.

"Ay, chihuahua, ay, chihuahua," Valentino cried as his aching body bounced and rolled its way down the steep stairs and landed...sprawled wide like a blob on the last step. "Ay chihuahua, ay chihuahua."

The Curious Mysterious Happenings of Valentino and the MYSTC Lions

Embarrassed, he looked around to see if anyone had seen his pathetic fall. When he was certain no one saw his dumb tumble, he pushed up onto four wobbly legs. Valentino gathered whatever pride he could find. He dragged his trembling body towards Max and Scooter.

"What was that pitiful noise?" asked Max.

"I'm not positive, but I think it's our buddy, Valentino," said Scooter.

They moved with caution toward their troubled friend.

They saw the bizarre vision staggering towards them. A wet and weak Valentino was so grateful to see his friends that he ran around in circles. Beads of sweat cascaded down Valentino's face... thick sweat flew in all directions as Valentino encircled his buddies. Between the storm of steam and Valentino's erratic behavior, it took time to get him settled down. His body was soaked and shaking uncontrollably. He continued to slip out of their grip. Finally they were able to tackle him. They sat on him to slow the mania.

"Valentino, what's wrong with you? You don't look good. Your behavior is odd, even for you," said Scooter.

"Ayúdame, ayúdame," said Valentino. "No me siento bien." He slipped into Spanish, his native tongue.

"Why are you so hysterical?" Max asked. "Has something or someone entered the house? Has the commotion outside started up again? Is the rest of the cat family okay? Why are you so wet?"

Valentino couldn't say anything useful. "No me siento bien," he repeated.

"I think he is saying he doesn't feel well," said Max the scholar.

As Max and Scooter focused their attention on Valentino, a determined Mamma Mouse covered her children. When the drama quieted for a moment, she peeked out from behind the chair.

"Come," Mamma Mouse said to her bloodied, crying children. "I'll help you get up the steps, away from the large cats. Hopefully we can find safety when we reach the top." She herded her little ones to the open stairway door. She was keenly aware of the danger that surrounded her and her family.

Alert to any movement from the mice family, Max saw Mamma Mouse and her children move furtively toward the stairs. He worried that Morgan, Wigs and Bean had come indoors and might see the mice on the steps. "Or worse," thought Max. "If Morgan sees the mice running across the floor, she won't be able to leave. Their day will be ruined and our day..." he shuttered at the thought.

"Maybe they'll stay outside," he hoped. "Oh boy, our day has just become more challenging. The mice will be harder to find in this large house when they get upstairs," he muttered...annoyed... worried.

"Max, help!" A frantic Scooter was shouting. "*He slipped free.*"

Max turned his attention to Valentino and Scooter. The chihuahua was running around the room again, trying to pick up and move whatever was in his way. He was acting so peculiar that Scooter and Max became deeply concerned for their friend.

When Valentino picked up a water bottle and raised his foot, Max and Scooter looked at each other. They dove for cover.

"Patada, patada," Valentino said.

From their hiding place, they watched in horror as Valentino launched the bottle with a mighty kick. He then fell to the floor, his eyes open. **He lay there, not moving.**

Max and Scooter ran to Valentino, fearing he was dead. When they reached him, they saw exhaustion on his face. "He's alive," the big cats shouted as they hugged each other.

"Valentino, are you well enough to move? Maybe we can help you up onto Aunt Jillian's bed?" Max asked.

"Thin sooo," murmured Valentino. In slow motion his words left his mouth, "I'm...feeeelin... verrrry...tured."

Aunt Jillian's bedroom was off the living space in the lower level. *Max had been banned from her bedroom due to attempted thievery. Max almost succeeded with his heist but the soft object of his pilfering was too big to get out of Aunt Jillian's room before he was caught. Max's need to drag and eat furry, fuzzy things gets him into trouble with everyone.*

Max the boss said, "Scooter, you carry his feet and I'll lift his head and shoulders. Together, we'll get him on the bed and under some covers."

Max remembered the ban on Aunt Jillian's bedroom, but the day had taken a serious turn. Mentally he was in Lion form now. Lions didn't do unimportant things like drag people's stuff to their water bowl.

They made it to Aunt Jillian's room and helped Valentino up onto the bed.

"Here's a wonderful blanket to snuggle in. We have things to do, but we'll check on you soon," said Scooter.

Max placed the blanket over Valentino.

"I...neeed...to...tell...you why I'm not...feeling...so good," Valentino said. "I..." Within seconds, Valentino was sound asleep. His words had turned to snores.

Max and Scooter quietly left the room...leaving the door ajar.

Once Mamma Mouse and her offspring reached the stairs, each mouse helped the others up the steps...with their mamma squeaking orders. As they reached the top step, she looked around at the unfamiliar surroundings.

She saw the perfect place to hide.

"Hurry, my babies. I know you are hurt, but I need you to move as fast as you can. Hold hands, follow me and stay close." With no time to waste, she hurried them to safety.

In her haste, she didn't notice the focused eyes of the WATCHER.

Chapter Five

"Tiny's Tale"

Tiny is a black cat with white boots. Tiny talks, but only by squeaking. She squeaks "hello" or "I'm hungry" or "I love you."

Tiny was born without a Meow Box.

She squeaks rapidly to say "I've got this ladybug cornered" or "come quickly" or "I know a secret."

She adores Valentino. Her comfort is knowing Valentino will protect her. They talk to each other. Valentino barks and Tiny answers with a squeak.

Because Tiny can only squeak, the other cats have trouble understanding her. Therefore, they tend to ignore what she tries to tell them.

Tiny focuses on her surroundings. She's aware of what is happening around her.

Today, she noticed five curious little creatures speeding past her and around the corner.

She knew they were scared. She knew where they were headed.

I remember a time when I had been scared. When I was just one year old, I ran through an open door in the house. I was curious where this opening would take me. But it was different from where I had come from and cold. I didn't know what to do. Nobody saw me leave, not even my cat family. And I couldn't find the open door so I could go back through it…back to where I had been where it was warm and humans and animals who loved me were near. I searched for that open door but never found it. Three weeks later, when I'd almost given up, my family found me. Today I stay away from any open door if I don't know what's on the other side.

Chapter Six

Aunt Jillian returned home while Morgan, Wigs and Bean were still outside. She saw that she had missed Mima but the car packed for the tournament was still there. "Good," she thought. "I'm not too late to see Morgan and the kiddos. She hurried into the house to change her clothes.

Jillian's bedroom was in the magnificent lower level of Villa Zoo. The generous space included a small kitchen. On her way to her bedroom, Jillian got a bottle of cold water from the refrigerator. She grabbed a glass and had a quick drink from the faucet...saving the bottle for later. Jillian put the glass with the unfinished water on the counter and hurried to her bedroom.

She passed Max and Scooter sitting on the sofa, looking at each other. Her bedroom was off the large living area where Max and Scooter seemed to be carrying on a conversation. "Silly of me, she thought. They look like they are talking to each other."

"Relaxing and dreaming," Jillian said aloud. "Must be nice to be a cat."

As she passed them, she noticed their eyes darting around the room. A new thought passed through her mind. "I don't think they are relaxed...far from it. And they aren't dreaming. Instead, they seem to be worried...anxious. What could possibly happen to cats who sleep all day to make them jittery...jumpy," she wondered.

She went into her bedroom and noticed Valentino curled up on her bed sound asleep. "That's odd" she thought. "He loves his doghouse. He never sleeps anywhere but there."

"Hmmm, I'm shivering from a puzzling energy coming from these cats," thought a rattled Jillian.

UNSETTLED...she changed her clothes, packed an overnight bag and left her bedroom. Valentino was still sound asleep. Carrying her bag, she headed to the steps...passing Scooter and Max on her way. The two were looking at each other. It seemed to Jillian that they stopped having a conversation when she walked past them. "No", she said to herself. "That would make me paranoid. These are cats." She hurried upstairs, feeling off-balance.

Morgan and her children came indoors from visiting the neighbors. The family was dressed and ready to leave. "Remember, your last but important chore is to get the animals settled in the lower level," Morgan said. "Get to it. We don't have much time before we meet the Wilsons."

"Come on, Wigs, help me," said Bean. "You find Valentino and take him outdoors while I check on the others." They hurried down the stairs, passing Aunt Jillian on her way up.

They shared hugs. Bean told her, "Mom would like to see you before you leave."

"I'll see her now," their aunt said.

"I know your mom wants it clean and *quiet* when she returns, but with five rascally cats and one dog with an attitude, I don't see how quiet relates to this bunch. They're not normal. Most animals sleep the day away...but not this gang," she said as she ran up the rest of the steps. She paused...turned and said to her niece and nephew, "I see danger around them all."

A hurried Morgan knew it would be late when they got home that night. "The house will stay neat if all the animals are together in the lower part of the house. If the doors are closed and they are confined to one space, maybe they won't get into trouble," she said hopefully.

Morgan saw her sister coming up the steps. When Jillian reached the landing, she hugged Morgan. "I'll be away for the night but I'll see you at the game," Jillian said.

"It's pretty hectic right now. We'll talk later," said Morgan.

"Downstairs," Morgan ordered as she saw Chai, Tiny and Yoshi strolling in from the bedroom.

She gently urged the cats through the doorway and down the stairs. "I wonder where the rest of the animals are?"

"Max and Bean," Morgan called down to her children. "Chai, Tiny and Yoshi are headed downstairs. Watch for them. I don't see Max, Scooter or Valentino up here. Please be sure they're already down there."

"Check their food dishes. They should have enough dry food for the day. Don't forget to fill the large bowls with cold water," Morgan directed. "Valentino needs to go outside before we leave. Very important." Downstairs, Bean and Wigs listened to their mom's orders. They waited for Chai, Tiny and Yoshi to come down the steps.

"Don't waste any time," said Morgan, urgently. "Oh, and don't forget your shoes if they're off your feet again. That's directed to you, Wigs. Make sure you close the door behind you...very important." At least the animals can't open a closed door, she thought.

Bean and Wigs together said, "Okay, Mom."

Morgan was still giving out orders but her words were fading in the midst of animal noises.

Bean and Wigs went about settling the five cats...starting with Max.

"Max," said Bean. "You're soft and fluffy. I love how big you are. I can't help but worry about you, though. You seem restless."

Max hates cuddling. He tries to run away when he sees Wigs come towards him. "Yuk," thought Max. "At least I got my glasses off and hidden before Wigs and Bean came downstairs. "I love them but they're nosy."

Wigs saw an opportunity to hold Max close. He took the heavy cat from Bean's arms. "I love cuddling you Max," Wigs said as he nuzzled his face into Max's deep fur. "You're like a giant pillow."

"Bah…ugh…double yuk," moaned Max, struggling to get out of Wig's grip.

Max was remembering the missing mice and needed the family to leave so he could set out to find the bloody babies. "I don't have time to play kissy face with Wigs".

All of a sudden, the pillow he was carrying earlier appeared in his imagination…along with a large, yellow water bowl.

Max laid back in Wig's arms, momentarily dreaming of his pillow. **Then he came to his senses.** He remembered the mice. He flew off Wig's lap.

Bean had seated herself on the sofa by Scooter. She hugged Scooter tight and said to him, "Be a good boy today, Scooter."

As Max flew by, Scooter left Bean's arms and joined Max. "Guess cuddles are not going to help these edgy cats," thought Bean.

"Because of their restless behavior, I'm not comfortable leaving them. Maybe they had a fight earlier. These two don't get along very well," Bean said. "And neither one bends to the other."

"I know," said Wigs. "They have a an odd relationship. Usually they hiss at one another if one threatens to get into the other's space. But today, they seem to want to be together…like they share a secret." Wigs remembered his earlier conversation with Mima.

Scooter, like Max, was anxious for the family to leave. They had mice to find and return home. Remembering the noises outside, Scooter thought, "Please let the mysterious sounds stay settled until our human family is gone."

Bean, distraught by Scooter's behavior, whispered to him. "I love you, Scootzie. Please, please be good."

As Bean reluctantly left Scooter, she looked over to see a hysterical Chai. Panic flashed on the face of the diva calico. A loud, piercing screech left her mouth.

Bean relaxed…smiled. Chai was being chased by Yoshi, who was in mischievous pursuit.

"Such a little diva," meowed Yoshi. He couldn't help but tease her. "You're no fun to chase these days. Your diaper slows you down."

Chai leaves poop pebbles whenever she's scared so Morgan makes her wear diapers.

The stairway door opened above. Morgan yelled down, "Come on, Bean, Wigs. We need to leave NOW. The Wilsons are waiting in their car. Remember to close the door behind you."

Bean stood up and walked to each window. She checked them all to make sure they were closed and locked. "There," she said to Scooter, "**now you have to stay inside**…if you left through an open window, there's a good chance everyone will follow you. We don't want that."

Scooter winked at Max…mischief radiating from his eyes.

Bean paused. "Scooter's a cat…but I think he just fluttered an eye," she thought.

"I don't see Valentino," Wigs said. "I thought he came down here earlier, but I don't hear him barking."

"Come to think about it, I haven't seen Valentino either," said Bean.

"Let's check Aunt Jillian's bedroom," Bean said. She was headed to her Aunt's room when she heard her mother's voice.

"NOW!" said Morgan.

Bean knew she was in trouble if she didn't get upstairs. She blew kisses to all her pets. "Be good," she said and followed her brother up the stairs. Both Bean and Wigs forgot Valentino needed to go outside to his Juniper tree.

They hurried past Yoshi...the tuxedoed contortionist. His legs outstretched, he was cleaning his belly while sitting up. They blew a kiss to Yoshi knowing he was lost in his world.

Tiny was in pursuit of some ladybugs crawling along the ceiling. Chai was under the sofa... hiding from a pesty Yoshi who had given up the chase.

"Bah, ugh," Max said as he and Scooter watched Bean and Wigs run upstairs. "I don't have time to lick Wigs' nose. I hate it when he cuddles me." Max made a face. He remembered the mice. Before he could do anything about the mice, he had to wait for the family to leave. He retrieved his glasses from their hiding place under the cushions. Max put them back on his face and adjusted them.

Scooter scratched his fur. "I need some alone time," he said as he thought of the faucet. En route to the kitchen, Scooter stopped. He paw patted his head. "The bloody mice," Scooter remembered. "We need to find them." Gone was the thought of cold water flowing alluringly out of a faucet.

Chai came out from under the sofa. Tiny left her beloved ladybugs.

When Max was sure the garage door had closed and all was quiet upstairs, he jumped up onto the sill of the window facing the side of the house. Once safely on the wide window ledge, Max looked outside. When the cars were out of sight, he turned and leapt onto the sofa.

As he joined the others, he noticed the open staircase. "Hmmm," he said. "Bean forgot to close the door."

Max noticed that Scooter had made his way to another window. Scooter used his big paws to unlatch it. "It's silly that Bean thought a locked window would keep Scooter in," thought Max as he moved quickly to stop Scooter.

Max's immediate concern was that Scooter was inviting more trouble into the house.

"Stop, bird brain," said a frustrated Max. "Think. The trauma those little mice witnessed outside earlier was more than babies who lost their mother. Something harmed them."

"They may have gotten in the way of a predator," said Max, his voice raised. "A hunter who might have had other prey in his sight."

Max knew Scooter...battle ready...would have his way. "Scootzie, if you have to open a window, please, for me, would you open it just a little?" urged Max.

Scooter agreed with Max's caution. "I can see your point, old man," he said. "Something is out there and until we can find the mice and get them to safety, we can't open the house to more threat. I want to be comfortable that our family is out of danger. Once we find the mice, we need to get them out the front door and home."

Scooter opened the window just enough to get some fresh air. He took a moment to enjoy a warm breeze on his face. Max nudged Scooter when he caught up to him. "We've got mice to catch old buddy."

"Let's alert everyone about the mice and prepare for our first step to become MYSTC Lions. Together we will execute the "United in Purpose" oath.

Excited about a new adventure, they were off to join the others.

The Cat Clan—Max, Yoshi, Scooter, Tiny and Chai—knew they would soon become the MYSTC Lions.

To engage in heroic combat successfully, one unbreakable union was required. Each cat will take the oath. When completed, each will become a Lion in Determination.

Step two was eating two Tuna Power Cakes...as one meal.

Max took charge.

A big ragdoll, grey and white in coloring, Max was considered the "Old Guy" in the family. He considered himself the wisest of the cats. A born leader, he designated himself Top Cat...Top Lion.

He told the others about the baby mice and Mamma Mouse. He told them about the blood oozing from the many sores on their tiny bodies. He told the others about the intense fear on the babies' faces.

"Scooter and I feel confident that the tiny mice were involved in what was happening outside earlier today. Remember the tornado like winds that blew the dirt in the air and shook the branches? Helpless animals were being attacked by some unknown beast. We don't know the size of this monster or how many there are."

Scooter continued. "We think the mice were the first victims. There is certain to be more suffering considering the terrified cries and the fierce growling we heard."

Max added, "We believe there was more than one predator causing this. Remember…Yoshi and Chai both saw something at the same time, but in different places. I believe there is something about the baby mice that is adding to their distress. I just can't identify what it is."

The animals were quiet, processing what they saw earlier and anticipating the hours ahead of them.

Then Yoshi spoke and broke the silence. "Where are the mice now?"

"While we were helping Valentino, the mice disappeared upstairs before Scooter and I could help them," Max said.

"What happened to Valentino?" Yoshi asked, concerned.

"We don't know," said Max, adjusting his glasses. "He fell asleep before he could tell us."

Scooter said, "He was really out of it for a while. He ran around in circles and was sweating. I've never seen him like that before today."

"I know this sounds odd," said Max, "but I think he tried to lift the sofa."

Some snickering was heard from the Cat Clan.

"At that point we hid but kept an eye on his weird, uncontrolled behavior," said Scooter. "It took some time for him to settle down."

"He continued to kick whatever was in his way. Then, he kicked a large water bottle and fell in a heap on the floor. Our confusion over Valentino's behavior turned to fear when we thought our friend had gone mad, or worse...that he was dead," said Max.

"We decided to put him down for a nap in Aunt Jillian's room," Scooter said. "That's where he is now."

"While he's sleeping," Max said, "we need to get back to solving the mice problem. They need to be found and returned to their home."

As Max was about to rally the Cat Clan to say the "United in Purpose" oath he noticed movement at the slightly-opened window.

Encircled by the direct sunlight and shadowed by the warm rays, was a form no bigger than a large potato. It had long, greyish-brown fur and big, round ears covered in dark hair. The ears had small hints of white at the edges. It had long whiskers and no tail—at least Max couldn't see one. "Maybe his tail was hidden in all that fur," Max thought.

Max noticed the wilted face and a frightened expression on the scared creature. He asked the others, "Are you seeing what I'm seeing at the window? I think it's melting before our eyes."

Chapter Seven

Max is a wary cat. But he sensed an urgency to get this creature into an air-conditioned house. Forgetting caution, he moved quickly down the sofa towards the window.

Yoshi said, "Bring it in slowly. Don't scare it, or it'll run away."

Scooter waved his paw towards the indoors. "It's obvious he's in need of the cool air inside Villa Zoo."

Max jumped to the window sill from the sofa and put out his furry paw to welcome their visitor. "Please," he said, still guarded. "Come inside…into the cool air."

The little mammal put out his front foot, smaller than Max's paw. His foot was densely furred on the sole. Max took the little creature's paw to guide him down to the sofa, but the frightened animal stopped and pulled back his paw.

"Please, my wife," he said as he pointed out the window to a small field of wildflowers near the Aspen trees. "Surrounded by the flowers is a rock. I placed her under it so the wild beast wouldn't get her. She was attacked by a giant animal that was after us. I don't know if she's still alive, but I can't leave her there."

"We are both pikas. Neither of us would ever hurt anybody. Please save her," he pleaded.

Moved by the animal's sorrow, Max opened the window just enough to bring their new friend into the cool air. Max called to the others. "Help me get a body buried near the Aspen trees. I want to bring it into Villa Zoo and the cool air."

At once, Scooter was by Max's side. "I'll help you, Max. Yoshi, Chai and Tiny, can you help us once we get the little animal through the window and into the house?" asked a heroic Scooter.

The others responded with enthusiasm...anxious to help. "I'll be waiting at the window. Just give me instructions," said Yoshi.

"Tiny and I will wait on the sofa with food and a blanket," said Chai. "And water."

"Squeak, squeak, squeak," agreed Tiny.

Max and Scooter went out through the window and into the backyard.

"Stay aware, Scootzie. Remember the screams we heard in the backyard and the foothills this morning? That fury can't be ignored," Max warned. "We're probably going to hit it head on."

"Mima was outside at dawn today enjoying the quiet at Villa Zoo. What caused the ground and the trees to rumble and shake so quickly after the quiet?" wondered Scooter.

"First, the bloodied mice. Now a ravaged body buried under a mound of grass ahead of us. We may be seeing a deadly end to this **Curious Mysterious Happening**," said Max, worried he and Scooter might be too late to save the female pika.

Scooter said, "The large black animal all of us saw was certainly at the center of the fury. We should assume he is still outside. Remember the conflicting accounts from the others? There's a possibility of two predators in the backyard of Villa Zoo."

Before they set out to rescue the injured female pika, they gave each other quick guy hugs.

"Here's to you, old man," said Scooter. "We've worked together through some dangerous times. I like saving lives with you by my side."

"Scooter, even though we didn't have time to say the oath, remember...we are united as we try to save this little girl. We are Lions in Determination."

"We have each others back, dude, oath or no oath. We'll work together and make it back with the victim nestled safely in our arms," Scooter said.

Together, they cautiously began the journey to recover the body lying under the rock at the foot of the mighty Aspen trees.

Yoshi and the male pika waited at the window, ready to help. Chai and Tiny waited on the sofa... supplied with the wet rags, blanket and food they had hurriedly gathered.

Yoshi, realizing the male pika might need water, asked Tiny and Chai to get some refreshment for him.

"I'll get it," said Chai, anxious to help. She jumped off the sofa and ran to the kitchen. Jumping up onto the counter, she saw the glass of water Aunt Jillian left earlier.

Chai put the glass of water between her teeth. She gripped it firmly with her mouth as she made it off the counter and onto the floor spraying her whiskers, eyes and nose with water. Undaunted, she ran to the sofa. From the sofa she jumped onto the window ledge.

When she reached the window, Yoshi took the glass of water from her and gave it to the grateful animal.

He drank all the water...happy for the kindness. Yoshi handed the glass back to Chai. After dry-wiping her wet face, Chai set the empty glass down nearby and ran back to wait with Yoshi.

Outside, Max and Scooter, always aware of their surroundings, advanced slowly toward the tiny figure laying deathly quiet under the rock.

They could feel eyes watching them as they moved forward.

Max stepped on a twig and it snapped. The noise thundered in the quiet. The leaves of the Aspen trees hummed.

"Just a little farther," whispered Scooter.

As they moved forward, pebbles rolled away hitting bigger stones and making louder noises.

"Easy does it," Max said. Finally, they reached the mound of grass. He brushed away the tall weeds. He lifted the rock and saw the lifeless body of a tiny female covered in blood.

"Oh boy," said Max. "I hope we're not too late."

"The beast really harmed this little girl," said Scooter. "Poor thing."

With care, Max and Scooter put their paws under her and pulled her out from under the rock and into the open air.

"We don't know what is lurking in the grove of Aspen trees," Scooter said in a concerned voice. "But something is there. I know it. I can feel its eyes on me."

"Let's get her to the safety of Villa Zoo," said Max.

As Scooter helped Max support the injured female, they heard spooky, chilling howls, followed by mind numbing screeching.

Max looked at Scooter. Scooter said, "We've just been spotted by the same animal that terrorized this little lady and the mice."

"I'm sure there are **two** of them," whispered Max.

Scooter looked up and ahead of him toward the Aspen trees. He saw the tall grasses move. Within the grove of Aspens, sunshine bounced off two moving black silhouettes. "Max, we are clearly in danger," said Scooter.

"We need to back up slowly," Max said, "I don't want the steps we take to encourage the animals to charge us. Then, let's calmly turn around and move forward to the window."

Scooter nodded in agreement.

Frightened for Max...himself and the helpless animal they were carrying, Scooter said, "I wish I knew what is hiding in the Aspen trees...watching us."

"What difference does it make?" asked Max. "Those are unfriendly growls and that's danger enough for me."

"What if it's Bull?" Scooter asked, thinking about Bitter GasBritches' dog. "He loves to threaten us."

Max whispered. "No, it's not Bull. It's shape doesn't even resemble Bull. We had definitive reports of two black creatures. I see the black forms, both with white on the tip of their tails. They are large animals and are baring their long, sharp teeth, which means they've spotted us."

After some thought, Max said "I don't think we are facing black panthers or wolves. I think we are being stalked by rare black coyotes. They are traveling together...which is unusual."

"In their eyes we are desirable prey...small and cats. If we were large like Bull and had noise makers, we could scare them away," said Scooter. "But coyotes drool over cats. One gulp and we're gone."

"That's an unpleasant thought..." scowled Max. "Let's move!" They backed closer toward the window.

"They are staring directly at us and will come down on us at any moment," said Max. "If we move fast, they'll move fast."

After they had backed up a little more, Scooter said, "We have several more steps to go before we are at the window. We need to turn around together, calmly. There's a danger of tripping over the twigs behind us, but we need to turn and face the window. We need to see how much distance we have before we reach safety."

Slowly they turned around to face the open window...and safety.

They moved forward...one careful step at a time.

"Don't trip over your big poly paws Scooter," whispered Max. Scooter winced, knowing Max had a good reason to say that. His paws were huge.

They hoped the small animal they were carrying stayed quiet. A moan from her might cause the coyotes to pounce.

With each painstaking step, they arrived closer to the open window.

Suddenly...a series of **howls** penetrated the air. Max and Scooter knew the coyotes sensed a change. The coyotes stepped out...away from the Aspen trees and into the clearing.

"Don't look back," said Max.

The coyotes stared directly at the trio in front of them. Drooling and growling through their teeth, they began stalking Max and Scooter. With each step the brave cats took, the coyotes followed with the same slow, precise steps.

Max and Scooter did not say a word to each other. In perfect rhythm they carried their precious cargo towards the open window. As they carried her, they protected her. Scooter with his large paws. Max with his furry body.

Max thought. "I've got to make a quick plan to protect Scooter and our little girl. If we do get attacked, I'll push them forward through the open window, protecting them with my body. When the coyotes reach me, I'll stall them with loud, whistling noises until Scooter is safe inside with the victim."

Max noticed that Yoshi was opening the window wider as they were getting closer.

At the same time that Max was planning how to get Scooter and the girl through the window, Scooter was thinking...coming up with his own plan to save Max and the victim. It was eerily similar to the plan forming in Max's brain.

"This is too difficult for our new friend to watch. He's shaking in fear. He may see his companion be lost forever to wild animals," whispered Scooter.

Yoshi, also concerned for the male pika, gently guided him over to the edge of the window sill. "You need to rest on the sofa and give us room to bring your wife to safety. We may have to move quickly," he said.

Yoshi helped the shaking little animal to the sofa. Chai gave him another drink of water. Then the pika, Chai and Tiny waited. "My name is Rocco," he said. "I'm frightened for my Hannah and the heroes who are trying to save her. We were followed...then chased by those coyotes."

Yoshi, back at the open window, watched on helplessly while Max and Scooter continued their slow walk to the open window...he watched the coyotes stalk them. All Yoshi could do was wait...wait for Max and Scooter to reach the opening and safety.

"I'm glad Valentino isn't here," Yoshi thought. "His barking would scare the coyotes into attacking." He glanced down at Tiny and Chai on the sofa. "Would one of you come up to the window to help me close it as soon as they get through the window?"

Tiny leapt up, ready to help Yoshi.

FINALLY...Max and Scooter reached the window. Yoshi prepared for the rescue. **ABRUPTLY**... his fear became a reality. *AT THE VERY WRONG MOMENT*, Valentino charged into the room barking for all to greet him...telling everyone he was back!

The coyotes, spooked by Valentino's barking, increased their speed. They lunged forward. Their dark, menacing eyes focused on Max and Scooter. The coyotes were ready to snatch them.

Seeing the new danger, Yoshi stepped outside to help when he saw Max and Scooter off-balance. He reached for the lifeless body.

Tiny tried to help Max and Scooter, who were both stumbling over one another in their attempt to help each other and the victim get inside. Heroes being heroes...but heroes who won't make it home without help.

Holding the injured pika, Yoshi ran through the open window and into the house. He jumped down to the sofa, gripping tightly to the precious female. He left her with Chai and Rocco, then ran back to the window to help.

Squeaking rapidly, Tiny flew through the open window. She ran behind Scooter and Max. Yoshi saw the two coyotes roaring down on their prey. The branches of the Aspen trees shook in warning. The hideous charging sounds from the coyotes electrocuted the air around Max and Scooter. With Tiny's quick guidance, Max and Scooter made it to the open window. She gave one hefty push, and the two cats dove through it. They were up in no time to grab Tiny and pull her to safety.

Both coyotes were within seconds of reaching them. Had the coyotes **NOT** run into each other in their wildly eager anticipation of a quick snack, at least one would have made it through the window and into Villa Zoo.

Tiny and Yoshi closed the window and the coyotes smashed into the glass. "Close call," gasped Yoshi. "Another second or two and they would have eaten all of us."

Max and Scooter breathed sighs of relief. Hearing the enraged noises from the two defeated coyotes, Max and Scooter watched as their prey angrily pawed at the window. Teeth bared and mouths drooling over what might have been, the predators finally gave up and turned away.

They limped back to the grove of Aspen trees...furious at being outsmarted.

"We'll worry about the coyotes later," said Max. "Chai, Tiny and Yoshi need our help." Max and Scooter jumped down from the window ledge and landed on the sofa.

Valentino watched, transfixed, as Max and Scooter flew through the open window. He saw the window close and the scary coyotes crash into the glass. He realized his barking had created more danger for his friends.

Feeling discouraged and sick again, he turned away from the horrifying scene in front of him and slunk up the steps to hide in his home. "I feel horrible knowing I put my friends into grave danger... **captured and eaten by the coyotes.**"

Reaching his home, he took some comfort from his blankets as he curled up inside them to rest his fractured heart and aching body.

He knew he needed to make a doggy trip outside but there was no one to help him. "Max and Scooter could get me out the door but they're busy saving lives," Valentino said, feeling sorry for himself. "I really need my Juniper tree."

Looking at the bloody, unconscious body lying on the sofa, Max noticed her appearance was similar to Rocco's. She was smaller in size but her belly was swollen. "She's pregnant," realized Max.

"With the heat, a coyote attack and a pregnancy, no wonder she's near death," Max whispered to Scooter. "We need to get more water and dry rags immediately. The cold water might revive her!"

Scooter headed to the kitchen with Yoshi. There they found berries, lettuce, grains, water, soap, and more clean rags.

Taking the rags to the sink, Scooter turned on the faucet while Yoshi soaked rags in the cool water. Then they placed the wet rags into a red, plastic bucket with a handle. Scooter grabbed the handle and moved quickly back to the sofa, while Yoshi carried the food in a bowl.

The cats washed Hannah, cleaning the cuts and rinsing the blood away. They put a cold rag on her forehead. They had water ready for her to drink if she woke up.

"Thank you," said a grateful Rocco. "I would not have been able to survive out there much longer. Hannah wouldn't have recovered if I had died. She would have perished under the rock...pregnant and mauled."

Rocco, thinking back to the danger he and Hannah had unwittingly wandered into, said, "Hannah slipped and bounced down the rocks as we tried to get away from the large black animals. They were focused on us and nothing would distract them. She was frightened of the coyotes. The heat wore on her body until she could go no farther. She landed on the ground and lay limp and quiet before me."

"I picked her up and hid her under the large rock by the Aspen trees," cried Rocco. "I was sure she had died in my arms."

"We had been picking berries and thistles and green plants to store for our food...and grass for the baby's nest. We didn't see or hear the coyotes until they were almost on top of us. By the time they spotted us, we had strayed too far from our colony. Luckily we were able to hide in the crevices of the rocks."

Rocco took a moment...overwhelmed by his experience.

"Instead of going back up the mountain to the colony where our families live," continued Rocco, "we were pushed farther downhill by the hungry coyotes. I knew if I moved us back up the rocks, the coyotes would follow us. I couldn't expose our families and the colony to those horrible animals so Hannah and I pushed on...moving down through the rocks and bushes toward your home."

"Hannah and I are American Pikas," he said. "Humans like to call us Rock Rabbits because we make our homes in the rocks high up in the mountains. We live in the alpine meadow above the treeline, keeping to ourselves and taking care of each other. We make our nests in the rocks where we also store hay for the nests and food for winter."

"Our families can only survive in the cold weather of the high elevation. Having foolishly strayed too far from home, we've struggled to survive in the heat down here," said a tired Rocco.

Max observed Rocco's appearance. He could see a weariness on Rocco's face but also strength and determination.

"Thank you for helping us...especially Hannah," Rocco said. "And for the water and the food. There are herbs and grasses outside that would build up our energy, but with the coyotes out there, we are safer in here. Hopefully they'll leave soon."

Scooter glanced out the window. "They're gone, but probably waiting for us...angry at being outwitted."

Rocco gazed at Hannah...his teary eyes became hopeful. Hannah was so quiet...but free of the rock and safe in the cool sanctuary of Villa Zoo.

A curious thought occurred to Max. He asked Rocco, "Did you notice any mice outside while you and Hannah were hiding from the coyotes?"

"Yes," said Rocco. "We were as afraid for them as we were for ourselves. The mice were screeching in high-pitched voices and didn't seem to have a good sense of where they were going. They ran every which way. They picked up speed as they were forced down the foothills. I think the cool air from your open window drew them forward."

"At that speed they became little balls, rolling down the hill until they were stopped by the rocks and trees near your home. When they stopped, there was silence. We thought they were dead," continued Rocco. "Slowly the mouse balls opened up. Soon their high-pitched screeching started up again. Running towards the cool air coming from the open window, they stumbled and bumped into each other. When they reached the opening, they disappeared into your home."

"Four young mice ran through our window a little while ago," Max said. "They were frightened and bloody, with cuts on their fur. Their mother arrived shortly after. She managed to comfort her children, but they've all disappeared somewhere upstairs. I thought there was something odd about the little mice, but I couldn't figure out what."

"I had that same thought when I saw them running into each other. They seemed to be guided by putting their noses into the air and following some sense of safety," Rocco said curiously.

"Your story explains why their bodies were all torn and bloody," said Max.

"Tell us how far you are from your home," Scooter said. "Now that you both have cool air, food and water, you'll regain your strength quickly. Hannah is young and healthy. She'll be okay...I'm now sure of that. Time and rest will help you."

"We have to find the mice and their mother first," Scooter said.

"After that, we'll come up with a plan to get you home," Max reassured Rocco.

Rocco teared up, happy they were safe and going home but sad for Hannah and the terror of what she just experienced. The coyotes had been determined to have them for a snack. He shuddered at the thought of what could have happened to his beloved Hannah.

Fighting back tears, Rocco needed to talk about the nightmare he and Hannah shared before their rescue.

"One of the coyotes stuck his nose down under the rock. He had our scent. We pushed against the rock, away from him...and waited. Then, he pulled his nose out and stirred the dirt to get us to come out. Frustrated when that didn't happen, he stuck his paw under the rock and snagged the scarf Hannah was wearing. He pulled the scarf, choking her. When he pulled the scarf out from under the rocks, he pulled some of her fur with it. She had a bloody hole where the fur had been," said an emotional Rocco. "The coyote was angry when all he got was the scarf so he pawed the rocks...again. I managed to get Hannah away by slipping through the lower rocks until we came out into the open air."

"I saw the open window. I pulled Hannah, trying to get her to safety," said Rocco.

"I can't go any further, Rocco. You go without me," she cried.

"Then she fell to the ground, limp. I thought I lost her. I picked her up and buried her under the rock." Rocco hung his head, tears falling down his face and soaking the sofa.

The cats hugged Rocco.

"Sleep, Rocco. You're safe here. Before the daylight is gone, we'll have you and Hannah home with your family," said Max.

Rocco laid down by Hannah. He closed his eyes and was soon asleep. His arms wrapped around her injured body...protecting her from any more harm.

"We have a busy day ahead of us," Max said as he took charge and quickly called the Cat Clan together. "Let's meet upstairs. Rocco needs sleep. Hannah will heal with sleep and the cool air."

Chapter Eight

Max paced around the room. He needed a hug from Mima. Maybe even a kiss on his crooked nose. "Mima loves my nose," Max was thinking. The others watched him with curiosity.

"Thinking about Mima and how I purr when I'm relaxing with her brings me clarity," Max reasoned.

He jumped to the window ledge...looked outside and felt the warmth of the sun. His eyes closed. Suddenly, his head popped up and he shouted.

"Finally! I know! Mamma Mouse's four little babies are blind!"

Pleased with himself, Max continued. "They can't be expected to behave as normal mice. We have to move forward expecting unpredictable behavior," said an excited Max.

"Yes," said Scooter. He paw patted with Max. "Mamma Mouse is frantic and even more protective because she has to be the eyes for her children.

"I wish we could help her understand we are her friends...that we want her and her babies to get home safely," said Yoshi.

"Our family will be home late tonight," Max said. "Even though it is still early in the day, we have a lot to do. I'm glad Mima is away but I know she'd be loving up our pika friends if she was here."

"Aunt Jillian isn't coming home tonight. That's a good thing because she's suspicious of what she calls the 'sizzling energy' in Villa Zoo," said Scooter. "She'd be nothing but trouble for us."

Max called for Scooter, Tiny, Yoshi and Chai's attention. "It is finally time to become *'United in*

Purpose'. Let's meet at the table near the kitchen."

One by one, each cat from the Cat Clan jumped up on a chair at the table and onto the table top. When all of the cats were sitting, facing each other, each one put up a paw. After several paw pats, the enthused cats vowed to become one united bond. In unison they said,

"I promise to stand by my fellow felines and be there to help them if they are in danger. I will do all I can to help our team reach the final goal safely. Throughout our mission I will move forward with continued purpose. I will never leave a Lion behind. I will act honorable at all times."

Following the oath, each cat felt empowered. Together, they became true Lions in Determination.

Max watched each one of his Cat Clan comrades. His eyes showed the pride he felt. Embarrassed by his emotions, the old codger cat grunted and said loudly, "Bring on the Tuna Power Cakes! A snack of two cakes for each of us will complete the TRANSMYSTC MUTATION...we will become the MYSTC Lions."

Cats love their Tuna Power Cakes. A snack of one round, delicious cake is an exciting part of their day. They love to sleep away the hours after one of the power cakes.

But **TODAY** they eat **TWO**! They become the MYSTC Lions! There will be no sleep for the mutated heroes!

"...There are mice to rescue and return safely to their home," said Chai.

"...There is a dog named Bull to fend off. An angry, giant, slobbering, sharp-toothed dog will be waiting outside...watching us leave Villa Zoo with the mice. He likes to **growl and howl** and **gnarl and snarl** at children and animals. He'll try to eat the mice...and then us! We need our strength to protect the mice and us from his massive paws and his raging temperament," said Scooter.

"...Two dangerous, rare coyotes are lying in wait for us," said Yoshi.

"...Two sweet, lost pikas are depending on us to help them get back to their family. We need time to plan the dangerous trip that will take us up to the top of the mountain. We'll be miles away from our home," said Scooter. "We don't know what dangers we will meet on our trip."

"Squeak, squeak, squeak," said Tiny, feeling powerful and, for once, understood.

"The **SUPER POWER STRENGTH** we need as MYSTIC Lions means two Tuna Power Cakes for each of us," said Max. "One delicious cake brings total peace. It prepares our bodies to fill up with the POWER from the second TPC".

All the Determined Lions agreed.

"The second Tuna Power Cake works only if it is consumed immediately after the first TPC," said Max. "Only then do we achieve TRANSMYSTC MUTATION.

"It puts the roar into our meows," said Scooter.

"It grows a mane around our heads and hair on our belly," said Yoshi.

"It puts the fierce into our cuteness," growled Chai.

"It makes our faces scary," said Yoshi. He put his hands to his mouth and said *"Aargh".*

"Our paws become large... powerful and furry. Our claws are sharp and long," Chai bellowed.

"Our tails grow long and become whips!" said Scooter.

"Our power swells," said Max. *"We go boom!"*

"Squeak, squeak, squeak," said Tiny, eagerness in her shrill tone.

Having declared the final step, the Determined Lions headed to the pantry to get the Tuna Power Cakes they had previously dropped to the floor.

Max and Scooter shared winks. Within moments, the desired cakes, hidden under a towel, would be theirs.

When they neared the pantry, Max stood tall as Scooter climbed up on Max's shoulders to shape the Cat Tower. They walked the Cat Tower to the pantry door. As Scooter reached for the door knob, he realized the door was slightly open. "Hmmm," said Max. "Did we forget to close the pantry door when we were interrupted by Wigs and his soccer ball?"

"The mice could have gotten through the opening thanks to your carelessness," said Scooter as he did a backward flip off Max's shoulders.

"My carelessness?" snarled Max. "My carelessness?"

They entered the pantry.

They both ran to the towel covering the cakes. With great anticipation, Max picked it up.

He pulled it open...he shook it...he couldn't believe it! The towel was empty!

"The Cakes are gone!!!" he shouted. He said to Scooter. "Quick, hop onto my shoulders. We need to check the Tuna Power Cakes we left on the top shelf."

Scooter jumped up onto Max's shoulders. Max swayed. Scooter swayed...but in the opposite direction. Scooter grabbed the shelf to steady himself.

Max's glasses fell from his ears and landed on the floor. Without thinking, he bent down to get them, leaving Scooter hanging from the shelf.

"Max!" Scooter roared. "This is no time to forget what you are doing. Catch me, quickly, you putz. I'm about to lose my grip."

"Scootzie, I'm sorry," said Max, apologizing for neglecting Scooter. "I'm upset about the missing Tuna Power Cakes. I can't imagine where they are...plus I lost my glasses."

He quickly moved under Scooter before the slipping big boy fell to the floor.

"So you think I'm not upset, Einstein?" asked Scooter, flashing his teeth...his ears *back*.

Recovering, Scooter said "Let's try this again. But let's keep our wits about us this time. Stay focused!" blustered Scooter.

Soon, Scooter was once again on Max's shoulders. Once balanced, they carefully maneuvered to the shelf where the other bags of cakes were stored.

As the Cat Tower was shuffling to the shelf, Max looked around. "I see no sign that the mice were in here. The floor is clean, except for the towel I gave you to cushion your earlier fall."

Once they reached the shelf, Scooter looked up. He dug his poly backpaws into Max's shoulders as he saw, with horror, that the shelf was empty.

"Max," Scooter shouted. "We have a problem!"

Scooter's shout echoed throughout the house. The other Determined Lions ran to the pantry. Max's shoulders were hurting from Scooter's poly paws digging into them. In pain he crumpled to all four paws, taking an angry Scooter down with him.

Scooter fell on top of Max. Together they laid flat on the floor, eight paws spread out like stacked pancakes.

After moaning and complaining, they finally got themselves upright onto all fours and looked at one another...both harrumphing.

"Scooter," Max said. "You dug your big paws into my fur and flesh. That's the second fall in the pantry today. Now, tell me, slow and easy...what is our problem?"

"The...shelf...is...empty," said Scooter in a controlled voice, anger seething...ready to explode.

"What?" Max shouted. "The shelf was full earlier this morning. And the fallen bag was under the towel. How could all those Tuna Power Cakes have disappeared within an hour?"

"This is a crime!" bellowed Scooter. "Today, **now**, we need the force from two Tuna Power Cakes... and there are none!"

"I know the mice didn't take them," said Max. "The pantry floor would be littered with scraps from the mice chewing through the packages. We would notice signs of tiny footprints. I don't see either."

"We don't have time to look for our precious cakes," Yoshi said.

Sadly, Max and Scooter agreed.

"Let's begin our search for the mice," said Max. "Before we know it, the day will be over and our family will be back. There's a lot of work to do to make everything okay before nightfall."

Valentino had finally fallen asleep. He felt sorry for himself because nobody had time to help him get outside to his Juniper tree. He woke up to Scooters' shout. Leaving his kennel, he wandered over to see what was going on. "What's all the fuss about?" he asked, yawning.

"Our important Tuna Power Cakes are missing," Chai said.

"We have no time to look for them," said Max. "Meet me on the floor by the chair. Form a circle and let's figure out where the baby mice and their mother may be hiding."

"Maybe I should help the cats," muttered Valentino. The devil in his grin and only a hint of guilt in his voice gave away his lack of desire to be of any help. Then he decided, "Nah, it's stupid cat stuff. I don't have the energy for this, and I still don't feel good. I'm going back to my kennel. I need to get outside, but nobody's going to help me now."

With an enormous struggle, he dragged his wet, shaky body and sickly tummy back to his private space. "I have many blankets to curl up in and lots of room to sleep," mused Valentino.

Once inside his home, he swirled and twirled and finally buried himself in his favorite thick blanket. Exhausted, he fell into a restless sleep and dreamt a tormented doggy dream. Once asleep, a portion of his blanket fell away, exposing an unusually puffy belly.

As the Determined Lions were discussing their first move in the search for the mice, Tiny, who was closest to Valentino's kennel, noticed him drooling on his blanket...a grin on his face. As Tiny moved closer to the large dog home, she noticed an alarming odor.

"Squeak, squeak," Tiny said. She was frantic...pointing at Valentino. Everyone understood she was warning them of an urgent problem.

Yoshi ran over to see what Tiny was squeaking about. Once he was near the kennel, he knew immediately. "Calling all Determined Lions! We better get Valentino outside to his favorite tree...and soon."

"Cat Tower," called Chai.

Max and Scooter got up from the floor and hurried over to the front door. Once there, Max stood erect and Scooter leapt onto Max's shoulders. In perfect harmony, they shuffled to the door. Scooter put his big poly paw on the doorknob. He was ready to open the door to the outdoors and Valentino's Juniper tree.

Chai, Tiny and Yoshi pulled a sleeping Valentino and one of his blankets out of his kennel. As the interior of the kennel became more visible, the Determined Lions couldn't believe what they saw. An opened bag of Tuna Power Cakes tumbled out with the blanket. Another bag was half-buried under one of Valentino's many blankets.

Chai, Tiny and Yoshi cheered and danced. Letting go of the doorknob, The Cat Tower gyrated in a circle, swaying their hips to hoots and hollers. Of course...they lost their balance and fell down. Max's glasses flew and landed on Tiny's face. Max and Scooter meowed and purred all the way down to the floor.

Once celebrating was over, they regained their composure and got down to serious business.

Upright on two hind legs, Max retrieved his glasses from a startled Tiny. He jumped up onto Scooter's waiting shoulders. "No daffy," said Scooter. "**I** jump up onto **your** shoulders. Remember? I have the large paws to turn doorknobs and grab stuff high up. Remember?"

"Just fooling," said Max as he helped Scooter up to his shoulders. "I'm so excited about the Tuna Power Cakes recovery that I actually feel playful."

Scooter rolled his eyes. "I didn't think you even knew what that word 'playful' meant," he said.

Once again, they made their unsteady way to the door.

Once the Cat Tower reached the door, Scooter grabbed the doorknob and said "Valentino saw an opportunity to go to the pantry. He must have been tempted when he found the pantry door open."

Remembering Valentino's behavior earlier that morning, Max said, "That's why Valentino was so sick and hysterical earlier. He ate a lot of the cakes! They made him sick! He's a dog, not a cat. Those cakes have the opposite effect on dogs. Cats become confident and powerful...dogs become weak and sickly."

"That's why his belly was so puffy," said Scooter. "It was full of Tuna Power Cakes."

Max wondered, "How did Valentino get up to the high shelf the Tuna Power Cakes were on? He must have a talent we haven't seen before."

Scooter pondered Valentino's feat. "That *move* I would love to have seen."

Chai, Tiny, and Yoshi continued to tug and push a drowsy dog toward the door and his favorite tree. Impatient with their slow progress, Max began tapping his feet.

Max and Scooter were an impressive height when they formed the Cat Tower. However, the wait for Tiny, Chai, Yoshi and a miserable Valentino was too long. Scooter decided to look outside, forgetting for a moment that Max was tapping his feet. He wavered too far and began, again, to lose his balance.

Out of control, Scooter swung backward, grabbing Max's face and knocking Max's glasses. The glasses slipped, hanging off one side of Max's head.

Scooter straightened, holding the doorknob with one hand, and adjusted Max's glasses with his free paw. "There, Max. I think we've finally learned this delicate art of balance," said Scooter. "And stop tapping your feet, dork. It's making me dizzy."

The steady Cat Tower opened the door.

Tiny, Yoshi and Chai had finally reached the opened door with Valentino in tow.

"How many cakes do you think Valentino ate?" Chai asked. "He's barely moving and I'm tired of dragging him."

Yoshi said, "I don't know about you two, but I'm exhausted."

Tiny was about to squeak her two cents when she stiffened at the sight of an enormous, snarling animal just outside the door, ready to charge into Villa Zoo.

Chai and Yoshi saw what Tiny saw. They dropped Valentino.

The stinky chihuahua said, "What's happening?" He tried to stand but fell into the open door, knocking it. Max wobbled, Scooter toppled...and the door flew wide open.

Chapter Nine

Valentino, fully awake, opened his eyes. He felt the breeze from the outdoors...which reminded him of his favorite tree...which reminded him of what he needed to do. As he stood in the doorway to begin the trip to the great Juniper tree, his body froze...his feet wouldn't move. Valentino was scared stiff by what he saw.

Framed in the sunlight stood a drooling, enormous dog. His bared teeth seemed bigger and sharper than Valentino remembered.

Valentino looked into the raging eyes of the giant dog. Eyes that pierced Valentino...daggers firing...veiled by a black mask.

Bull had deep mahogany coloring. He would camouflage his large body in the bushes...wait for Valentino and the Cat Clan to come out of the house. **The door opened! The cats appeared...peeked out!** He left his hiding place! He sensed action! **Bull crouched...stalked the yard to the front door.**

His head was huge...overshadowed by a wrinkled forehead. Bull's long legs covered a large area quickly.

He reached the open door just as it flung open.

Bull couldn't believe his luck.

The salivating animal was ready to pounce. He grinned...his mouth stretched wide. Bull glared through the open doorway...focused on his target.

"Helloooo...Valentinooooo," he said in a low...slow...burning voice.

A stiff Valentino shivered.

Bull lives with a man known to the Cat Clan and Valentino as Bitter GasBritches. Bitter GasBritches is feared by all the children in the neighborhood. Only Bull loves him. They share the pleasure of tormenting children and animals.

Bitter GasBritches is a tall, looming man. He wears his unruly, wiry hair in a long ponytail. His glasses are black. Through the lens his sinister, angry eyes threaten. GasBritches moves with a distinct limp.

Crows survive in the deadened forest surrounding GasBritches' home. Green leaves and flowers die as they begin to bloom. Towering trees hide the sunshine but allow endless darkness to penetrate the house of Bitter GasBritches and his dog Bull.

A young man, GasBritches wears a black shirt, jeans and high rubber boots. When he speaks, he grunts. Animals and children are frightened by his creepy behavior.

Bull resembles a small, brown pony. He is thick. His paws dig holes in the grass as he awaits the arrival of the Cat Clan and Valentino.

"Patience pays off," snarled Bull...his face contorted in anger. He bared his teeth as he pawed the ground with anticipation.

Yoshi looked around, searching for any sign of Bitter GasBritches. Not seeing the mean man... he breathed a sigh of relief. "We just have Bull to get past right now. He looked at the others. With six of us and one of him, we can do this...right?" asked a nervous Yoshi.

Valentino needed to get to his tree. He stopped being frightened and started planning...all the while focusing on the movements of the unpredictable dog in front of him.

"It doesn't seem right that my friends have to face this danger because of me," thought Valentino.

An excited Bull moved forward...cautiously.

Suddenly...he raced forward...spurred by the opportunity of capture.

"He's moving fast," thought Valentino.

The giant dog was advancing straight toward the Cat Clan. Bull will soon be face-to-face with all of us. "He's not going to stop," reasoned an anxious Valentino. "If I don't do something Bull will be in the house. My friends and our guests are in fatal danger.

With seconds remaining, he knew what he had to do.

Without further thought, Valentino leapt onto Bull's back!

At first startled, Bull recovered quickly. Wanting to get the pest off his back, he turned away from the house and bucked fiercely around the yard. As Bull went through a maze of bushes, Valentino hung on for dear life.

"I hope Bull passes my tree soon," thought an anxious Valentino, his eyes darting across the yard...looking for his Juniper tree. He couldn't believe he was riding Bull.

Bull had other plans. With Valentino still on his back, he ran across the street to the home he shared with Bitter GasBritches.

"Oh, no," Valentino grumbled. "Now I'm in real trouble. I can't do anything but hang on to his black bandanna."

GasBritches was outside when Bull arrived with Valentino on his back. "Well, well, what have you brought home, Bull? "Bitter asked. Snickering, he said, "Looks like you found a friend."

"Please," Bull whined. "Help me get this thing off my back. I've done everything to try to get rid of him. It's like he's stuck with glue! I've run through the bushes and leapt into the air. I've run in circles so fast that I made myself dizzy and still...he's on my back."

Of course GasBritches didn't understand what Bull was saying...but he read the whining quite accurately. Poking fun of Bull, GasBritches said, "The big, mean dog is crying."

Hearing this, Valentino was emboldened with bravery.

"I thought I'd taught you better. If you can't remember my simple lessons, then you're on your own," GasBritches said. He turned away from Bull, went into the house and slammed the door. GasBritches never looked back.

Dejected, Bull continued to leap and buck. He ran back to Valentino's yard. "Maybe another run through the bushes will finally rid me of this pest," Bull thought.

Valentino hung on dearly to the black bandanna. His newfound bravery gave him the nerve to peek over Bull's head. He couldn't believe it! Coming up was his beloved Juniper tree!

"It's now or never," said Valentino. He let go of the bandanna and flew off Bull's back, landing near the tree.

Bull, not realizing that Valentino was off his back, continued to buck, circling the yard. Valentino quickly did his business. He looked for the leaping Bull. Valentino began the trek back to Villa Zoo and the open door as fast as his four short chihuahua legs would carry him.

The Determined Lions watched from the open doorway. When Valentino disappeared for a while, they were worried. "What are we going to do if Valentino doesn't come back," asked a concerned Chai.

"Maybe that horrible dog ran away with him," Tiny was saying. All that her friends heard was "Squeak, squeak, squeak."

"What if Valentino is lying injured somewhere and needs us?" asked Yoshi.

"Let's keep cool heads," said Max. "If we don't see Bull and him soon, we'll need to go looking for Valentino."

"Look," said an excited Scooter, pointing. "Here comes Bull. Can you believe that Valentino is still on his back?"

Excitement and pride radiated from Valentino's five friends. They watched in awe as the chihuahua expertly jumped off Bull's back, and did his business. They watched with concern as Valentino began the long run from the Juniper tree to the house and the open door.

Valentino neared the door. The Determined Lions stepped out to help him through the doorway. Valentino...his legs spinning...shot past them and into Villa Zoo. Gliding through the open doorway, he landed on his belly, his four paws stretched out...and sailed into the living room. A sigh of relief that Valentino was inside Villa Zoo...the Determined Lions closed the door.

Bull, realizing Valentino was not on his back, turned in time to see the white chihuahua with the kisses collar fly into the house. He raced towards the open doorway. The door shut on Bull's charging bulk...abruptly dismissing the enraged Mastiff.

"Phew," said Valentino, pulling up to stand on all fours. He shook with relief. "I believe I narrowly escaped Bull and his teeth. He's a vicious dog, and wouldn't think twice about gnawing on me as he would one of his bones."

A recovered Valentino told them about the trip to Bitter GasBritches' home.

"Oh Valentino, you're so brave," said Chai, swooning over her friend.

The Determined Lions fussed over Valentino with lots of hugs. They couldn't stop praising him.

Tiny, who adored Valentino, squeaked and rubbed her face on him.

"You were fearless," said Max. "A real hero." The Determined Lions looked at each other and nodded. They all agreed Valentino was a brave dog.

"We want to ask you to become an official Lion. You are someone who seizes...not hesitates... when the time comes to save someone from harm," said Scooter.

"You acted quickly...you knew what to do," said Max. "I think you saved us all from the unthinkable harm that wretched dog would have done to us."

"We could use your help with the Curious Mysterious Happening behind Villa Zoo," said Yoshi.

"Thanks, but no thanks," said Valentino. "I'm content to be there for you, my friends, whenever danger is near. But if being a Lion means eating those awful Tuna Power Cakes, I'd rather not be an Honorary Lion."

He yawned. "I'm sorry for taking your unique power cakes."

He returned the half-eaten bag to Max...plus the full unopened bags recovered from under a different blanket. "I took the Tuna Power Cakes. I knew they were important to you but I was thinking of myself. I'm sorry I caused you anguish."

Feeling much better after the trip to his tree, Valentino walked his tired body to his large kennel and dragged it into his home.

"I'm warmed by Valentino's apology," Max said, "Let's sit by our brave buddy until he falls asleep."

The Determined Lions gathered around Valentino's very large kennel.

Valentino twirled and whirled and was soon burrowed under his favorite blanket. A loud snore was heard coming from the kennel…followed by several bellowing waves of snores from the mouth of the sleeping head that peeked out from under his blanket.

His friends nearby…a job well done. Valentino fell into a deep sleep.

Max whispered to the others, "Let's go to the dining table to enjoy our Tuna Power Cakes and complete our TRANSMYSTC MUTATION to become the MYSTC Lions. Be quiet as we leave Valentino's home…we don't want to disturb him. He earned his favorite pastime…a long nap."

With bags of the important Tuna Power Cakes gripped tightly in his large poly paws, Scooter led the journey to the dining table and their final passage.

When they reached the table, they climbed onto the chairs and put their paws on the top of the table. Scooter and Max handed out the crucial Tuna Power Cakes.

"Remember" warned Max. "If we wait longer than five minutes after finishing the first TPC, we won't mutate. Our bodies will lose the peace created by the first Tuna Power Cake and will no longer be pure enough to receive the power released by the second TPC."

"Enjoy the first one. When everyone is finished with the first TPC we'll eat the second one right away," instructed Max.

Each Determined Lion took small bites from the first Tuna Power Cake. They loved the tuna taste.

The first and largest bite brought great happiness.

The second bite thrilled and tickled.

As they ate the third bite, tears ran down their faces.

When they ate the fourth and final bite, the tears were gone. Each Determined Lion was full of peace.

They allowed themselves a moment before beginning the second critical Tuna Power Cake.

"We have a lot to do once our new, altered selves leave this table," said Scooter.

"Our journey to TRANSMYSTC MUTATION has begun," roared Max.

"Our second TPC is the final step to mutation. The power and energy we generate will get us through the search and rescue of the mice. It will carry us and our friends...the pikas...up the Rocky Mountains and back to their families. We have hard, dangerous work to do before darkness."

"Take this final Tuna Power Cake." Max handed it to each Lion in Determination. "Enjoy it any way you please. We wait together until every cat takes his last bite," said Max.

They ate in quiet.

They thought about what super power means to them.

They will soon fight danger as the MYSTC Lions.

They finished their last bite in unison.

They smiled at each other.

Then...
Lightning snapped.
The table shook.
Slow-moving magic neon bullets sprinkled
  down onto the five brave Lions.

They growled.
They roared!
Their fur grew long.
Their chests expanded and their front legs grew powerful.
Their sweet faces grew fierce.
Newly slanted eyes focused on what had to be done.
Faces elongated as the nose expanded to meet a widening mouth.
As the mouth opened to roar it showed sharp, pointed teeth.
The tail grew long and strong as a whip.
The spreading paws became woolly...masking sharp claws.
They took in the potency of their power!
The toughness of their strength!

THEY WERE SUPERHEROES!

When all was quiet and the heavens closed, they stared at each other. What they saw reassured them that the mutation was complete.

"Together, we are the strong, brave MYSTC Lions. And now, we have a courageous Valentino as our loyal sidekick," said Scooter proudly.

"He's brash. He'd gladly pass responsibility to others in order to get in a good nap! He won't willingly check out trouble...but when the tough moments come, he's there for us," agreed Yoshi.

"I don't think he'd hesitate to take risks when the situation called for quick action," said Chai. "He deserves a good rest."

"He's the first one to take on Bull...and win," said Max as he leapt onto the kitchen counter and grabbed some of Bean and Wigs' brain putty. "Here, catch!" he said as he threw the brain putty to each of his fellow Lions. Four flying lions left the table and reached high to catch the brain putty. "You can work it with your paws as we discuss the next job," roared Max. They each caught the brain putty like pros and began to knead it.

The time to plan for the rescue of the mice had arrived. They began a serious discussion with one objective...success!

Pushing and pulling the brain putty helped the MYSTC Lions get mentally prepared. Adrenaline pumped their enthusiasm.

Throughout the kneading and the planning, Tiny was frantically squeaking out words. The others had no idea what she was trying to say.

"I'm sorry, Tiny," Max said. "We want to understand you but don't. This is a crucial situation. We are running out of time."

She continued squeaking. The Lions...regretfully...continued to ignore her.

Tiny manipulated her brain putty with the others. She knew what was happening and understood the plans. She continued squeaking.

"If only they could understand me, I could save them precious time," thought Tiny. "I'm a WATCHER. I see things."

Soon they put the brain putty aside.

"First, we should discuss the behaviors of mice...the food they eat, where they hide when they are scared," said Max.

"Please keep in mind that they are hurt," Max continued. "The cuts on their bodies from rolling down the hill have not been tended to...except by their mother."

"They would want to be wrapped in something soft to make their wounds less sore," said Chai. "Maybe we should look for them in towels or blankets."

"What might encourage the mice to put aside their fears?" Yoshi asked. "Mice are curious." Then Yoshi's furry face lit up. "Maybe they're hungry! What would they eat?"

"The young mice would probably still drink milk," Scooter said. "We could soak some bread squares in milk and hope Mamma Mouse would carry a soggy bread square to her children."

"Remember," Max said, "they came into our home to get away from the coyotes, not because they thought it was safe here. They went from one problem to another. They are blind. They have only their senses to guide them...and their mother."

Chai shook her head and added sadly, "Their journey is not over."

"If we use food to bring them out into the open room, how will we offer the food to them? We are cats who look even more threatening now that we are the MYSTC Lions," said Scooter in one of his rare thoughtful moments. Scooter was a fighter and a doer...he left the thinking to Max. "Mice don't like us or trust us...and even though the babies won't see us, their mother sure will. She's the one who'll look for food."

"Hmmm, you're right, Scooter. Once we decide on where we think they may have hidden, we should place food around that area. Then we'll hide, of course," said Max. "They may grab the food and return to their hiding place, but at least we will know where they are."

"We can't keep a window or door open to the outside for them to run through. We've got Bull on one side and the coyotes on the other," said Yoshi.

"We could scare them out into the open. I'm not happy frightening them but seeing the mice would give us a chance for capture. If they were captured, we could get them to their home promptly," said Chai.

"Good thinking everybody," Max said. "Do we all agree that we use food first to find them? If that doesn't work, then we use fear to bring them out?"

Together...Yoshi, Chai, Tiny and Scooter nodded their heads.

"Yes," Max thought, "the brain putty did its work for the MYSTC Lions."

"Squeak, squeak," said Tiny, trying one more time.

"We love you, Tiny, and we know that you're part of the discussion," said Scooter, "but time is not on our side right now. We know you understand everything. I'm sure what you have to add is important, but we can't take the time to figure it out."

"Okay, Lions, let's discuss where we think the mice are hiding. It might be worthwhile if we narrow down their hiding places to two or three possibilities. They were scared when they reached the top of the stairs...they only had their mamma's eyes. She would have had to physically guide them to safety. I think she would have led them to a place near the stairs," reasoned Max.

"They may have burrowed into something deep and soft because they are scared and sore," said Yoshi. "The hiding place would have to be large enough to hold five mice and soft items for burrowing."

"Great reasoning, Yoshi," said Max.

"We should limit our discussion to rooms near the top of the stairs," said Scooter.

"I think the laundry room, kitchen, living room, and nearby bathroom are the most logical places to hide," said Chai.

"Let's try to narrow this down. Scooter and Tiny, take the kitchen. Yoshi, take the laundry room. Chai, the bathroom. I'll take the living room," said Max. "Report here when you're finished. We'll figure out our next move from what you each have to tell."

When each Lion reported back to Max, they reviewed the possible hiding places.

Scooter and Tiny felt the kitchen was not a suitable hiding area.

"We looked under the sink. It's too full of supplies to hide five mice. Plus, there were no visible rags or towels to hide under. The drawers are closed tight. We didn't think four blind mice could have made the climb to hide in the drawers," reported Scooter.

Yoshi had a different report.

"The laundry room is a possibility," he said. "There's dirty laundry and clean laundry waiting to be folded. There are many towels on the open shelves. Plus, we can close the door for easy capture," Yoshi said.

Chai reported what she had found in the bathroom off the laundry room. "All the cabinet doors are closed. They could have settled in the waste basket because there is tissue inside, but I lifted the basket and shook it. I listened carefully but didn't hear any noises. I checked the shower. The door to the shower was shut, so they couldn't be inside. I don't think the bathroom is a good option," said Chai. "However, I kept the door open in case we wanted to direct the mice there if we find them since it's not a large room."

"That leaves the living room," said Max. "The sofas and chairs have thick cushions. The entertainment center has a couple of open shelves, leading to the back wall. There are several loose pillows on both the sofa and oversized chairs. The window seats have blankets and pillows, but I don't think the mice would have been able to climb up there. They were under pressure to find safety quickly," reported Max. "I checked out all the possibilities."

"So that narrows the hiding areas to two rooms. Let's focus on the laundry room and the living room...and hope we're right," said Chai.

Max was about to discuss the next step when a horrifying thought occurred to him. "Bull and Bitter GasBritches are probably outside, anxious to play out their own evil plans. Bull is probably even more furious now since he was outsmarted by our little chihuahua buddy."

"If they see us leaving with the mice or the pikas," Scooter said, "Bull will want to include them in his plans for dinner. Stay alert, Lions," he instructed the others.

"After we find the mice and capture them, we'll figure out how to get them out of the house without Bull attacking us," agreed Yoshi. "But we're getting ahead of ourselves. Let's find them first."

Max called everyone to the dining table. "We've agreed to use food as our first step in capturing the mice," he said.

"We know we will focus on the laundry room and the living room," said Yoshi.

"We've agreed that we'll use food in key spots. We'll hide out of sight so Mamma Mouse doesn't get suspicious," Max said.

"She'll run back to feed her children...revealing their hiding place. We'll grab the nets for a quick capture," said Chai.

"Good idea, Chai," Max said.

"Before we move ahead with our plan...Yoshi, will you and Tiny bring in the nets from the garage and put them in the kitchen."

Yoshi and Tiny ran to the garage.

"Scooter, you and Chai go downstairs to check on Rocco and Hannah. Let's make sure they are okay and are continuing to recover."

Yoshi and Tiny returned with the nets. "The nets are ready for a quick capture," Yoshi said. "We've placed them near our hiding place."

Scooter and Chai came back with big grins on their faces. "Rocco and Hannah are sleeping peacefully. They've got their arms around each other and their bodies have cooled off!" said Scooter.

They didn't wake up," Chai said.

"While you were gone, I was considering what food we have that will bring Mamma Mouse out of her hiding place," Max said. "We have food in the pantry."

"Cat Tower," roared Max as he made his way to the pantry door. Scooter followed Max. With Max standing erect, Scooter hopped up onto Max's shoulders. He turned the knob of the pantry door. Moving slowly, they pulled the door open and maneuvered the Cat Tower into the pantry. The Cat Tower shuffled to the pantry shelves.

Scooter grabbed a peanut butter jar and dropped it to the floor. "Peanut butter on the fly...watch out below," warned Scooter.

"Watch out for my paws!" said Max, wondering why it had to be such a big jar of peanut butter.

Tiny, Yoshi and Chai waited below to take the food from the pantry to the table.

Upon hearing Scooter's warning, the three MYSTC Lions wisely scrambled out of the way. Hidden under the lower shelf, they watched the peanut butter jar fall to the floor. The lid opened and flew off. It landed on Yoshi's large lion paws.

Down rained a cereal box, a jar of nuts and a box of crackers.

As the opened can of nuts fell, it sprinkled it's contents onto the floor...flooding it with peanuts.

Yoshi's lion ears deafened from the noise of the falling food. Tiny squeaked complaints. Chai, always edgy due to her diva nature, peeked out from under the lower shelf...a towel covering her furry lion ears.

Once all the food was on the floor, Chai tossed the towel signaling a go ahead to the others.

They left the safety of the low shelf and entered the middle of the pantry into the minefield of bombed food. Three MYSTC Lions gathered the food. They pushed, dragged, and carried it to the table.

As Scooter flipped off Max's shoulders and landed on the floor, he said, "The baby mice may want milk. The idea to soak bread squares in the milk is worth trying."

"Scooter," Max roared. "We can get milk and bread from the icebox. Let's move the Cat Tower to the refrigerator. You lower the supplies to me, and I'll give them to Yoshi."

Max took his glasses off so they wouldn't fall from his face. He handed them to Chai who returned from the table. Scooter and Yoshi joined Max. Scooter jumped up onto Max's shoulders. Balanced, he opened the refrigerator door.

"I see the milk! Fortunately, Morgan bought a small carton of milk," Scooter said as he grabbed it with his paws and handed it down to Max.

"Here, Yoshi," said Max, handing him the milk.

Yoshi pushed the milk to the table.

"I have to stand on my toes to reach the bread. I have to stretch, aaaa, aaaa," Scooter grunted. "I can touch it. Just a little farther...there, I have it! I have it!" Scooter said gleefully as he pulled on the bread wrapping.

"I'm not sharing your joy, Scootzie," said Max. "I'm slipping to the floor because your big lion paws are digging into my shoulders and I can't see because your tail is covering my eyes."

"Yikes!" Max said as he went down muttering something about how he was glad his glasses weren't on his face.

Faithful Yoshi, waiting below for the bread, saw falling Lions above him. Knowing they would land on him soon, he roared and ran. Yoshi narrowly escaped harm as he took refuge behind the pantry door.

Scooter, a loaf of bread in his paws, fell down from his lofty position and landed on the bread. "Well, it's a little smashed, but I think I can get some squares from it to soak in the milk," he said as he dragged the flattened bread loaf to the table.

"Are you okay, beefhead?" Scooter asked Max when he returned to help Max up from the floor.

"Harumph," Max said as Chai handed Max's glasses to him. "We've got to get better at this, ChumpNinny," he said sarcastically. Both of the big lions forgot their vow of team spirit and unity. "I'll meet you at the table." He grumbled as he strutted over to the others, holding his furry head high to mask his damaged pride.

The noise in the kitchen woke Valentino up with a start. "Is someone robbing the house? Where's everyone? What are those horrible, loud sounds?" he said sleepily.

When he didn't get an answer, he pitter-pattered over to the activity at the big table. He watched his friends making food trays. They dunked crackers in peanut butter. They chewed up nuts to a size the mice could eat.

He noticed their appearance. "Whoa," he thought. "Those are some pretty serious dudes. I'm seeing first-hand that my huge, hairy friends are playing for real."

The MYSTC Lions quietly prepared the food at the table. Focused on their immediate goal, they were aware that Valentino was watching them...fear and awe on his face. His skinny tail wagged fiercely. His little body jumped up and down, fueled by anxiety.

On small paper plates, they placed tiny nuts, cereal grains, and crackers smothered with peanut butter. On a separate paper plate, they placed small bread squares smothered in milk. All during the preparation, they listened to Tiny's squeaks...more insistent now. She was driving them crazy.

"Why is she so frantic today?" wondered Max. "Could it be she's trying to tell us something we need to know now?"

They carefully lowered the filled plates to the floor and pushed them to the living room and the laundry room. When all the plates were in place, they ran back to the kitchen and hid. Watching from their well-chosen hiding place...they were able to see both rooms.

They watched and waited...in capture position, ready to move.

After an agonizingly long time, they relaxed their capturing position. No longer watching...they sat and waited a while longer...listening.

Discouraged...they had to agree that no mouse was coming out to eat. Not even hunger was bringing out Mamma Mouse or her babies. Not a squeak was heard.

"This is a tough case," Scooter said.

Chapter Ten

The room was quiet as the MYSTC Lions reflected on the failure of the feed and capture plan.

"Let's move to our fear option. I know we don't want to scare them, but I don't see any choice. If fear doesn't work, there's no option left for a quick capture," said Scooter.

"Maybe we were wrong on where they chose their hiding place," Chai said.

"That thought is too overwhelming to consider yet," said Max. "We have a good second choice. Let's move ahead with our plan to scare them from their hiding place."

"We have nature's advantage on our side. Mice are frightened by cats. They'll surely be frightened by Lions," said Scooter. "We should be able to make enough noise to make Mamma Mouse move."

"Since we are brainy Lions, we need to use our intelligence to organize another well-thought out plan," said Yoshi, his lion paw rubbing his brain.

"Let's start in the living room and put out our best chorus of hisses, snarls and low growls," said Max. "We can push our noses into possible hiding places. Snort and sniff. Retreat...find a new hiding place. Continue to hiss, snarl and low growl. Push our noses once more into another potential hiding place. Again...snort and sniff. Retreat...continue the hissing, snarling and low growling. Put a paw into the hiding place...move the paw around. Retreat again but roar with even louder noises."

"That should shake them up...frighten them. Without thinking, they'll run out into the open. They'll be frantic trying to find safety," Yoshi said.

"Yes, that's a good plan," said Max. He was saddened that they had to add more fear to these sweet little creatures' lives but they had to take extreme measures in order to get them out of Villa Zoo and back to their family.

"When we see them, with our quickness, we can jump onto their tails and capture them," said Chai. "Max and Scooter will build the Cat Tower and open the front door. We'll all rush outside, tails in our mouths, and return them to their family. If we're fast, we can beat the coyotes."

"Let's alert Valentino so he can distract Bull. Every one of us might have a good chance of surviving if we work together," said Yoshi.

"I saw Valentino watching us, so I know he's awake," Chai said as she went off to find their buddy.

With enthusiasm in the air, Valentino was already making his way to the MYSTC Lions. "I heard your plan," he said to Chai. "I think it's a plan that will work. You can count on me." He turned and, with purpose, walked to the front door, ready to do his part.

"Once we're out in the woods," said Max, "we'll make sure our little friends are safe. When we are certain we weren't followed by Bull or the coyotes, we'll make a dash back to the house and through the open door."

"If Valentino climbs onto Bull's back, Bull may run around...distracted. That'll give us time to get to the woods with the mice," said Yoshi.

"When he sees us return to the house, Valentino can jump off Bull's back. When Valentino is in the house, we'll close the door in Bull's face. Maybe Bull will finally get the message," said Chai. "We **CANNOT** be taken down. We *are* the MYSTC Lions."

They all agreed it was their best plan yet. With great enthusiasm and enormous confidence, the MYSTC Lions put their plan into action.

From the living room to the laundry room, they whooped their best hisses, snarls, and roars.

They pushed their noses into every possible hiding place. They snorted and they sniffed. Large furry paws went into small spaces and moved around, certain to scare anything alive. For a long while they continued their hunt with their loudest and best hisses, snarls and roars. The house thundered with a MYSTC Lion chorus.

Eventually, the chorus quieted. No mice squeaked. No frightened faces peeked. Mamma Mouse never showed up to sass the MYSTC Lions.

When their noses were bruised and their snarls and roars fell to whispers and their paws hurt, the MYSTC Lions gave in to defeat.

"How could we have been so wrong about the places they chose to hide in? Are they buried so deep in this big house that we will never find them?" Max asked.

"I'm worried about the mice. I wonder if they died from their injuries. Poor Mamma Mouse. She must be paralyzed with fear," said Chai.

Valentino, equally dismayed by the failure of the fear plan, returned to his kennel. "I can doggy dream away any happenings quite well," said Valentino. He opened the door to his large kennel and began to dig a tunnel into his blankets.

The discouraged Lions watched a defeated Valentino walk to his kennel. They were heading to the table to discuss their next move when a piercing cry fractured the air.

"Mira, mira," Valentino cried. "Ay! Ay!" Then an odd dance took over his body.

"What is he trying to tell us with that weird dance?" asked Yoshi. "And why has he slipped into his native tongue?"

"He is telling us to look at his kennel," said Max.

"Mira, mira," Valentino repeated, too shaken to bark. He continued to prance his chubby chihuahua body around in circles. Then he stopped and unloaded several more piercing barks.

He pointed at his blanket. "*My blankets*," said a trembling Valentino. There was no sign of the bravery the MYSTC Lions had seen earlier. He moved away from his kennel, closing the door behind him, saying "No puedo creer que me haya acostado con ellos en el mismo espacio."

While Valentino freaked...up popped four blind mice faces and one very angry Mamma Mouse. The mice squeaked, too frightened to run.

Stunned...the MYSTC Lions watched.

"They must have seen Valentino's kennel door open and the kennel empty. Encouraged by the warmth of the sunshine and Valentino's blankets, Mamma Mouse considered it a good hiding place," said a recovered Chai.

"A wise Mamma Mouse. She knew they would feel better in the heat from the sun. The soft blankets would protect their wounds," said Max.

"Valentino was downstairs so it became an excellent hiding place," said Yoshi. "I bet we'll find one or two of the Tuna Power Cakes still in the blankets."

"With the dog house as large as it is, the frightened mice could burrow deep under the blankets and stay on the far side away from the door," said Scooter. "Valentino was not feeling well today so our attention was on him. All the mice had to do was stay hidden and be quiet."

"Quick," Max said. "Now that the mice are safe, we need to move swiftly to get them outside."

They roared with fresh enthusiasm, "We are the MYSTC Lions!"

The MYSTC Lions sprang into action.

Max and Scooter made their Cat Tower at the door. Valentino and Tiny pushed the kennel while Chai and Yoshi pulled it, quickly making their way to the open door and safety for the mice.

When the three Lions and one dog arrived at the open door with the kennel and the mice, they pushed the kennel so it faced the outdoors.

With a mighty heave by all, out the front door and down the steps bounced one large kennel full of blankets, four squeaking blind mice...and a shrieking Mamma Mouse.

Three flying Lions followed the tumbling kennel. Valentino kept watch at the open door.

Max and Scooter broke down the Cat Tower and joined the other Lions. They left the door ajar so getting back into the house would be easy.

The MYSTC Lions looked around.

No sign of Bull.

No sign of the coyotes.

No sign of Bitter GasBritches.

BUT BULL WAS THERE...a shadowy figure hiding in the bushes.

He saw the chaos at the opened door.

He sensed victory...a tasty thought.

He moved quickly...taking long leaps toward the group.

Bull slowed his pace...awed by what he saw. "The cats look threatening. They're bigger and have claws and fur on their faces. They'll put up a good fight if I try to eat them. In fact, they don't look that tasty," thought Bull.

Then he saw Valentino. Spurred on by his earlier embarrassment, he forgot the lion-like creatures in front of him and headed towards Valentino.

Valentino saw Bull coming. When Bull reached the entry, Valentino leapt onto Bull's back as a challenging Bull charged the entrance. "It worked before, hopefully Bull isn't any smarter this time," thought Valentino.

"Not again," thought Bull. "How could I be so stupid a second time?"

He ran through the bushes and across the street to Bitter GasBritches' home. Seeing a frantic Bull, Bitter came out of the house, clearly disgusted with Bull's whining. "Bull, this is your problem. Figure out how to handle this pest who's no bigger than your paw, or don't come home again." He went back into the house.

Bull returned to Valentino's yard with tears in his eyes.

Valentino hung on dearly to the black bandanna, his little legs bouncing high every time Bull bucked.

Valentino's bravery gave the MYSTC Lions the opportunity they needed.

Earlier in the week, Max had seen mice in the woods. He knew they had claimed that part of the foothills as their own. He felt comfortable returning Mamma Mouse and her blind babies to the wooded area on the side of the house.

The MYSTC Lions headed toward the trees with the kennel, but kept their guard up in case the coyotes were lurking...waiting for them.

"Let's hope the coyotes remained in the Aspen trees behind the house," said Max. "I think Bull and all the noise he's making alerted them."

"Because Bull is bigger than they are the coyotes may not have wanted to take a chance," said Scooter.

The MYSTC Lions listened for any low growls, but neither heard nor saw the rare black coyotes. They each took a corner and carefully pulled the soft, cozy blanket from the kennel. But as the shaking mice felt their temporary home moving from the safety of the kennel they burrowed deeper into the blankets.

The MYSTC Lions dragged the blanket until they were far into the wooded area. Once they reached the protection of the trees, they unwrapped the cover. Mamma Mouse and her four blind mice peeked out. The babies stared with wide eyes, sensing familiarity.

"I just saw Bull trying to buck Valentino off his back. Bull was barking. Valentino was howling," said Max. "Bull kept leaping into the air, trying to rid himself of the biggest reason he was having a miserable day."

"Thanks to Valentino, we were able to get the mice home," said Yoshi.

Slowly, the mice moved away from the blanket. Mamma Mouse, gaining confidence, gathered her bloody and bruised children and gently guided them to their home. Mamma Mouse, her arms around her babies, turned to the MYSTC Lions. With glistening eyes, she waved good-bye to her new friends. "Thank you," she squeaked.

The MYSTC Lions watched until the mice disappeared. They left the woods for home, dragging the blanket behind them. "Well done, mate," said Scooter to Max as they fist bumped paws.

Max, thinking of Rocco but still wary of the coyotes, stopped long enough to grab a few blades of grass. "Same to you, Scootzie," said Max. "We may get into each other's way, but as MYSTC Lions... we're good together."

Max and Scooter joined the others. The MYSTC Lions gathered all of Valentino's blankets and the kennel. Working in harmony, they hoisted the kennel up into the house, and pushed it to Valentino's favorite spot. They put Valentino's many blankets inside his kennel and waited for him to come home.

Tiny squeaked nonstop. It was then that Max realized Tiny probably saw everything. "Tiny was trying to tell us where the mice were hiding," said Max. The MYSTC Lions surrounded Tiny and lifted her on their shoulders and threw her into the air. Furry body with tail flying...Lion paws outstretched...

Tiny landed gently onto the sofa. They praised Tiny. She smiled and squeaked happy squeaks.

"Tiny must be the only Lion in the world who doesn't roar," snorted Scooter.

Valentino noticed his friends had made it safely back to the house and began trying to find a way to get off Bull's back.

"Yeow! What is happening?" shouted a startled Valentino as the earth rushed to greet him. He realized Bull was laying down.

Valentino jumped off before he was crushed under the giant dog.

A confused Valentino stared at Bull...he saw that Bull was crying. Not delicate, gentle teardrops, but thunderstorm and lightning sobs. He couldn't leave Bull. Instead, he sat down next to Bull's face and tried to lick his tears.

Bull looked at Valentino. Through the tears running down the football size face of this monstrous dog, Valentino saw a smile begin to spread over the sad face.

Having successfully rescued the mice, the MYSTC Lions were overwhelmed with relief.

"We still have one more major task to solve before daylight becomes nighttime," said Max.

"Our pika friends are rested and ready to see their families," said Yoshi.

"We need to consider our trip," said Max. "We have rocks to scale and trees to wrestle. We could run into wild animals who can hide under the tall woodland growth. A mountain storm can hit us at any time along with severe lightning."

The Curious Mysterious Happenings of Valentino and the MYSTC Lions

"We'll have to climb 5,000 feet or more," said Scooter.

"The sun will be hot and there's no breeze so we'll need a lot of water," said Chai. "We're strong enough to make the trip but we need to be fast also. Mountain lions are quick."

"Someone will need to carry Hannah, and another MYSTC Lion, probably Scooter, will need to carry Rocco. They're too little and will be too weak from the heat to make the trip on foot," said Yoshi.

"Someone will have to carry the water," said Scooter. "And we'll have to have someone carry medical supplies."

"This will take all of us," said Yoshi.

"Squeak, squeak," said Tiny, letting everyone know she understood.

"Since we all will take this trip up the mountain, we need to figure out how we can stay close so no one gets separated," said Max.

"Also, and this is important if we are to survive this dangerous trip, we need to figure out the best action to take if we run into wild animals. We don't know where the coyotes are," said Chai. "We could run into them on the path to Rocco and Hannah's home. There are mountain lions to avoid, if possible...and black bears!"

"This is going to be a big undertaking," said Max. His long skinny tail was flipping uncontrollably as he was speaking. This happens when his energy is unleashed in big spurts! Tiny decided to sit on Max's tail while Max was talking.

"Not to mention, a potentially deadly one," Max continued. "We have to watch over each other. I wish there was an easier and safer way to get Rocco and Hannah home." Max sighed, thinking of the danger his MYSTC Lions would face.

The MYSTC Lions realized Valentino had not yet returned to Villa Zoo. Alarm spread through the group. They listened at the door but heard nothing.

"We have supplies to pack before we start up the mountain," said Scooter, returning to the discussion. "We have to plan how to secure both Rocco and Hannah for a safe trip up the craggy, steep hillside. We'll be facing a mountain full of danger at every turn."

"We can't start out until we know Valentino is all right," said Max.

Tiny, Chai, Scooter and Yoshi all agreed.

"Stay by the door until we hear Valentino barking. If we don't hear from him soon," Scooter said, "we'll go looking for him."

While Scooter, Tiny, Chai, and Yoshi waited for Valentino, Max fixed a plate of the grasses with some berries from the refrigerator, and took the mixture to Rocco and Hannah. Both pikas were awake.

At first they were alarmed by Max's appearance and shrunk back into the cushions. Max quickly realized how different he must appear to the pikas. "Please don't be alarmed. Our bodies are ready for the energy, strength and speed we'll need to get you home."

Reassured that Max was still Max behind all the fur, they smiled and took the food he offered them.

Hannah gave him a big hug. "Thank you," said Hannah.

"You're welcome, Miss Hannah," said Max the charmer.

Centering his attention on Rocco, Max asked him, "Rocco, do you remember the path you were on before you realized you were lost?"

"I think so." Rocco told Max about the mountain area where he and Hannah lived, and about the rocks or taluses, as the rock structures were known. The pikas make their home in the rocks.

"We live beyond the treeline, where trees don't grow. There's a meadow there. That is the beginning of where our colonies call home."

Rocco turned to Hannah and said, "I've searched beyond the boundaries the pikas are comfortable with. These boundaries are set for the safety of our hard-working pika colony. Pikas are always searching for food to store and materials to use for building nests."

"But I've had this urge to see what's beyond the safe borders of the colony. My mother said I'd see trouble someday if I didn't stay close to home. I guess she was right," said Rocco. "And now I've endangered you and the baby."

"Don't worry. We'll get you back home to your families," said Max. "You can't change what has happened, but you can learn from it."

Rocco told Max the path the MYSTC Lions must take to reach the pika colony. When he and Rocco finished talking, Max went upstairs to see if Valentino had come home. As he reached the top step, he heard the familiar, irritating bark he knew well. It was followed by a giant howl.

"Valentino is home," said Max, "but something is different."

The MYSTC Lions looked at one another...concerned. With trepidation, Max and Scooter made the Cat Tower. As the others watched with a puzzled expression on their faces, they slowly opened the door.

A bucking duo bolted through the doorway and into Villa Zoo.

Scooter and Max, unable to stay balanced, tumbled to the floor and onto the other MYSTC Lions.

Valentino rode on top of a bouncing Bull...who had a grin on his face so big, it practically hid Valentino.

The unlikely couple narrowly missed the pile of Superhero Lions.

Pandemonium charged through the house, an uncontrolled energy filled Villa Zoo.

Max, the first to recover, couldn't believe what he was seeing. A bouncing Valentino was riding on the back of a frisky Bull...the huge dog actually looked happy.

Scooter, having pulled himself out from under the pile of fur, was in the path of the canine tornado. "Dive," Scooter said as he dove under a table.

Tiny, Chai, and Yoshi picked themselves up from the floor. "Squeak, squeak, squeak," said Tiny.

They saw Bull and his rider headed for them.

"Fly," Yoshi said as she, Tiny, and Chai sailed over the sofa in time to avoid being trampled.

Bull ran into a chair, and it landed sideways on the floor. Valentino flew off Bull's back.

Bull screeched to a stop on the carpet. He saw Valentino crumpled on the floor. Bull went to his motionless friend. He nuzzled Valentino, whimpering until the small dog with the white kisses collar moved. Bull, his tail knocking a lamp and a vase to the floor, dropped down to lay next to his buddy.

"Valentino, I'm sorry. I don't know my own strength," said Bull. Whimpering and drooling, Bull continued to nuzzle his new buddy.

Max surveyed the mess. "Now we've done it. Morgan will send us all packing if she sees this messy room." He shook his head at Valentino and Bull.

Valentino regained consciousness. He struggled to stand up aware that Max needed an explanation...fast.

Valentino, wet from a slobbery licking, shook off his fall and began to explain how he and Bull became buddies.

"I was a nuisance on his back," he smiled. "Bull ran to his home hoping this time Bitter

GasBritches would help him. Do I need to mention that Bitter GasBritches is one miserable, grumpy guy? Sorry, Bull."

Valentino continued. "Bitter didn't want to help him. He slammed the door in Bull's face. I was going to jump off his back and run home. I knew you had rescued the mice. But, I just felt so sorry for the big dog."

"We left Bitter's home and crossed the street to Villa Zoo. As we neared the bushes, Bull slowed down, then quickly dropped down. By then I knew his fighting spirit had seriously weakened," Valentino said. "I thought I should stay with him. I was quiet and watched his face. I wiped away some tears. Then he started to talk."

"Valentino, you are the bravest little dog I have ever met," said Bull. "It warms my sad heart that you all unite to help each other."

"Bull told me he didn't like being mean," said Valentino.

"Being mean to children and animals makes me unhappy," he said.

"Would you help me be nice?" Bull asked. "You could ride on my back any time. I don't have any friends," said Bull, tears running down his huge face.

Valentino, his big heart warming with love, said, "You could begin by being true to the kind of dog you really are. You don't want to be mean, so don't be mean."

"I'm your friend, Bull," said Valentino. "I'll always be your friend."

Bull licked Valentino's tiny head. He jumped up, careful not to hurt his new buddy. "What can I do to help my new friend?" an excited Bull asked.

Valentino thought for a minute. "I have an idea that would help all of us. We could use someone with your speed and size to help us get two new friends back to their home on the mountain top."

Bull jumped up onto all fours. He broke into a happy run...around and around in circles, barking loudly. "I would love to help you...just tell me what to do!"

"We need to hurry home to the MYSTC Lions to tell them you'll help. It'll make a difficult, dangerous trip easier," said an excited Valentino.

"So here we are, ready to help," Valentino said as he finished his story. He saw the dewy eyes of his buddies as they listened with admiration to Valentino's story.

"That is a wonderful story, Valentino. And yes, yes, yes we can use Bull's help!" Max said. "And it will make the trip easier."

"We were very worried about you. You continue to make us proud with your bravery in the face of danger, your kindness to others and loyalty to your friends. You are one of us and you don't ever have to eat a Tuna Power Cake," Max continued.

The others nodded their heads in agreement.

The MYSTC Lions gave Valentino and Bull their best paw pats.

"Scooter," said Max, "let's go downstairs to get Rocco and Hannah. They can come upstairs to rest on the soft sofa pillows until we have our plans finalized and we're ready to leave."

Downstairs, Hannah and Rocco were scared by all the loud barking and noises they heard upstairs. Rocco, worried that danger found them again, made plans for an escape.

When Max and Scooter arrived downstairs, they saw Rocco and Hannah, fear on their faces, lowering themselves to the floor.

"Rocco," Max said, "Don't be alarmed. Everything is okay. In fact, better than okay. Valentino found someone to help us. His name is Bull. He's a large dog and he's upstairs. He is noisy and that's what scared you. But he's our friend and your friend."

"He's strong and fast on his feet. He'll help get us up the mountain and return both of you safely to your home," Scooter said.

"Scooter, Bull and I will take you and Hannah to the mountaintop," said Max. "Hannah, climb onto my back."

Relieved, Rocco helped Hannah up and onto Max's back.

Scooter lowered himself so Rocco could climb up on his back.

"We're ready," Rocco said, after he looked at Hannah and she nodded.

Max and Scooter walked to the stairs. Careful not to lose their precious cargo, they took each step with care. Rocco and Hannah held on tight. They finished the climb and reached the top step.

Scooter and Max walked to the comfortable sofa.

Rocco jumped off Scooter's back and helped Hannah off.

Hannah and Rocco scurried up to the sofa pillows and nestled in.

Chapter Eleven

The MYSTC Lions worked together to get ready for the trip up the mountain to take the pikas home. With Bull's help, the MYSTC Lions will reach the pika's home with speed.

They packed a small backpack with supplies. Max tried on the sunglasses he found in a bag of old swimwear.

They decided not to take food as it might attract the coyotes or bears that live in the mountains.

"Scooter and I are planning to take Rocco and Hannah home using Bull as our transportation," Max said to the other Lions.

"We have a lot to do here to get the house clean while you're gone. Morgan was serious about an orderly Villa Zoo when she returns," Yoshi said. "As Lions we can get this place clean in no time."

Tiny agreed with several squeaks.

Max found some thin rope and made a halter for Bull and reins for everyone to hang onto during the trip. They found three small pillows to make a saddle for each to sit on. Rocco and Hannah would share one pillow.

"We can protect the pikas by putting them between us. Our supplies can ride on Bull's side," said Max.

"Now that we know how we'll get up the mountain, we need to talk with Rocco about where we pick up the path we should take. I'd also like to know where the coyotes first spotted them," said Scooter.

They joined Rocco at the sofa. Rocco said, "There's a meadow not too far from our home. Once we pass the meadow, we'll make it home. There are many pikas in that area, but you won't see them because they live underneath the rocks. It's important for you to know that once the pikas sense our approach, they will bark to warn the others of approaching danger. Almost immediately, they'll band together to ward off trouble, so we should be quiet in the meadow. **When we hear the warning barks beginning, you need to leave.**"

He looked at Hannah, then he looked at Max and Scooter. "We may not get a chance to say goodbye, but we want you to know we are grateful. Without your help, Hannah would not be alive...and the coyotes might have eaten both of us. I know we won't see each other again. But on a still day, listen for my squeaking. You'll know it's me, because our squeaks don't usually reach far away—but mine will be extra loud. I'll call to you from a large, high rock."

"We'll **all** wait for your call Rocco," said Max.

Bull was thinking about the journey they had ahead of them. "We may meet bears or coyotes on this trip so we need to be ready to protect ourselves," Bull said, coming close to the sofa. "Find an empty soda can. Fill it with stones. We stand a chance if we're watchful. Noise will chase away coyotes, cougars, bears or any other wild animal if they don't get us first."

Max, Chai and Yoshi went into the garage. After some digging, Max found an empty soda can in a basket in the garage. He handed the can to Chai and Yoshi.

"There are some small stones in the garage. Would you fill the soda can halfway with the stones while Scooter and I get the halter and reins fitted to Bull's head?" said Max.

Soon, Chai and Yoshi returned with a can that sounded like a loud noise machine.

"That will do the job," Bull said, holding his ears.

Chai and Yoshi helped Max and Scooter put the halter and reins over Bull's head. Bull was so big, the Lions had to jump to the top of the table to reach his head. Next, they tied the pillows to Bull's back and around his belly. Max tugged the pillows...reassuring himself that they wouldn't slip.

"I'll put the noise maker in a backpack and attach it on Bull's side. It will be easy for me to reach if we see the coyotes, mountain lions or black bears that roam the Colorado Rockies," said Scooter.

"We can't trust the mountain lions to see us and automatically assume we're their friends just because we look like them. They might consider us their enemies," said Max.

"I'm glad we have plenty of light for this trip. We should make it back before the sun goes down," Scooter said. "Unless we run into some serious trouble."

Before mounting Bull, the travelers drank enough water to keep them hydrated for the beginning leg of their trip. When Scooter was on Bull's back and comfortable on a pillow, Rocco jumped up and helped Hannah get safely positioned on the pillow. The other Lions helped nestle them between Scooter's strong back legs.

"They'll stay safe burrowed in your furry body," said Yoshi. "And those huge paws will catch them if they start to slip off."

Max jumped up front, taking Bull's reins. His glasses slipped from his right ear. Scooter used a paw to adjust them for him. "Thanks, furry buddy," Max said.

The Curious Mysterious Happenings of Valentino and the MYSTC Lions

"No problem, big old cat!" said Scooter as he placed the noise maker into the backpack. Max couldn't help but give a roar as he turned Bull around and headed towards the outdoors.

Two MYSTC Lions, a giant dog, and two pikas said good-bye. The outside door had been left slightly open so they could leave the house. Tiny opened it wide enough to let them out.

"Keep this door ajar so we can get back in when we return," Max said.

"Villa Zoo waits for your safe return," said Yoshi. The MYSTC Lions who remained at home saluted the travelers and roared their goodbye. They watched as the massive dog and his brave riders disappeared.

Once outside and alert to danger, Bull took them behind the house to find the path Rocco and Hannah had used. Once on the path, Bull began the climb up the steep mountain.

His speed and endurance on the steep slope and over the rocks pleased the Lions.

Scooter whispered in Max's ear. "We're lucky Bull is doing this for us. We're fast and tough and could make this trip on our own. But Bull's size and speed will get us to the top of the mountain and the meadow in a shorter time."

"Bull is serious, self-assured and focused," Max whispered to Scooter. ""It's hard to believe he hated us. Worse, that he wanted to eat us."

"Bull's furry paws are tough but he's going to test that toughness today. Let's stop on the way back to refresh with cold water from a stream and check Bull's paws," Max continued.

Bull began running up the mountain. The Lions continued to be impressed with his speed and agility.

Hannah and Rocco were excited they would be seeing their families soon.

Time passed. They enjoyed the gentle breeze, the slight rustling of the leaves and the warm sun.

"No hint of a thunderstorm yet," thought Scooter.

Suddenly Bull stopped.

"What do you see, Bull?" asked Max.

"On the path directly in front of us is a rattlesnake," said Bull. "I've stopped moving. I'm backing up slowly, so he won't lunge at us. He spots us, though. He's coiled, ready to strike. Hear his tail rattling? This unusually large rattlesnake is a danger to us if he strikes my leg. By backing up, I'm letting him know we aren't here to hurt him."

The rattlesnake began to slither forward, uncoiling himself as he slithered rapidly toward Bull's legs.

"Guess he isn't getting the message," said Bull as he moved backward with more urgency and speed.

"There's also a snake hanging from the tree!" shouted Max. "He could drop on us at any moment."

Bull continued to back away from the charging rattlesnake. The rattlesnake lunged and Bull tripped. Everyone hung on as Bull struggled to regain his balance. The rattlesnake took advantage of the dog in trouble and made one final lunge. "Hang on," Bull shouted. He raised his legs high in the air and jumped over the attacking rattlesnake, narrowly missing the one swinging from the tree.

The hanging rattlesnake slithered down. He dropped to the path to join the other one. Looking back, Bull and his riders saw the rattlesnakes, heads turned, watching them. They had taken ownership of the path but had not stopped Bull.

Up and over the rocks Bull took his riders. When he reached a fallen tree, he carefully crossed over while Scooter held the pikas and Max controlled the reins. After traveling over rough terrain for what seemed like a long time, Bull spotted another path. He followed the new path with the smooth dirt. It felt better on his paws as they continued their trip up the mountain.

The Curious Mysterious Happenings of Valentino and the MYSTC Lions

Eventually, Bull stopped. Scooter pulled out cold water for everybody. He gave Hannah and Rocco drinks...then Scooter and Max refreshed themselves. It was Bull's turn...he guzzled water...drooling and grunting after each enormous gulp. Bull handed the remaining water back to Scooter for safe keeping.

As Bull began to move forward to continue the climb, he noticed bear tracks. The tracks were heading up the mountain. A black bear had taken the same path the travelers were following.

Bull continued on the path, watching the bear tracks. He noticed smaller tracks alongside the larger tracks. After climbing a short distance, Bull became certain that the black bear had a cub with her. He stopped, not wanting to continue until he knew if the mother bear and her cub were nearby.

"Why have we stopped?" asked Max.

Bull said, "I think a black bear and her cub are somewhere near by. I've been following their footmarks but the impressions stopped moving forward and have left the trail. Stay quiet for a moment," Bull instructed.

They listened for any unusual sound.

"I think I heard some growling over to the left near that large rock," said Bull. He focused on the area where the growling came from. He saw a small black head peek out from behind a tree. Bull was sure it was watching them! A small black bear emerged from his hiding place behind the tree and began confidently walking towards Bull and his riders.

"Yikes," swallowed Bull. "We don't want to be anywhere near that little black bear...as cute as you think it is." Bull started backing away. "It's the cub and you can be sure, his mom is nearby. That cub is not afraid of us because he knows his mother will protect him," Bull whispered as he looked around frantically for the large mother bear. Max and Scooter stayed focused on the cub.

Suddenly...Rocco eeked several rapid, anxious sounds. Max looked to where Rocco was pointing. He saw a large mamma bear walking toward them. The giant bear stood up on her two back feet and growled loudly. Back on all fours she woofed and barked...shaking her head wildly and scaring animals around her.

She wanted Bull and the Lions to know she was protecting her baby.

With the cub on one side and the big female bear on the other, Bull finally knew exactly where to back up.

After he had backed up several feet, Bull barked, "Scooter, remove the noise maker **NOW. HURRY!**" Scooter grabbed the soda can with the stones. Bull rose up to stand on his two back feet. "Now, Scooter! Shake that can and don't stop."

Bull's riders hung on dearly!

Scooter handed the noisemaker to Max. He shook the soda can continuously. Bull barked and snorted and wheezed. Together, they made as much noise as they could while Scooter held onto the scared, shaking pikas.

Mother Bear watched her cub while keeping her eyes on the travelers. Her curious cub stopped to watch the tension between its mom and the intruders. Mother Bear moved toward her cub. With every step she took to reach her offspring, Bull backed up, continuing to bark and growl. Max continued to shake the soda can.

When she reached her cub, Bull continued to keep his eyes on her...not sure if she'd chase him and the Lions or stay with her cub. Bull backed up. Mother Bear didn't move once she reached her cub.

Slowly, Bull continued backing up until the distance between him and the large bear was far enough that Bull could turn and run.

He continued running up the mountain until Scooter asked him if he needed a rest. He wanted to make sure he and Max weren't becoming too heavy for Bull.

Bull, his heart pounding and his adrenalin spiked, was elated to have outdistanced the bears. "I have extra energy. Don't worry about me. We are close to our destination."

He continued to climb the mountain, taking his riders up the path toward the treeline and just beyond to the meadow and the pikas' home.

Soon, they reached the treeline. "Trees can't tolerate the cold beyond this elevation, so we should see the meadow soon," said Rocco. Within minutes the familiar meadow came into sight. "The rocks, where we make our home, are just beyond the meadow."

The group fell silent as they passed through the grassland. Rocco whispered, "Stay quiet. We're approaching our home. I'm hearing faint barking. Soon it'll grow louder."

The others heard the faint alarms, too.

They continued to travel in silence.

"We should leave you now," Rocco said in a hushed voice. "We can make it from here. Thank you, my friends. We'll always remember you."

Knowing the pikas needed to move fast, Bull stopped. Rocco removed himself and Hannah from the security of Scooter's big paws. The two hopped off Bull's back. Taking Hannah's paw, Rocco led her across the meadow to the rocks and their home. They stopped, turned for a moment and waved goodbye to their friends. Then they were gone.

Bull and the Lions continued to wave until their friends disappeared. Quietly the two MYSTC Lions and one large, smart dog turned and headed down the mountain slope until they were below the treeline.

"We needed your help, Bull," said Max. "Your speed and intelligence were crucial to successfully getting the pikas home. Thank you." In response, Bull did a leap in the air. Scooter and Max roared, almost falling off.

Loping towards home, the trio filled the hills with whoops and roars...Rocco and Hannah were home.

They enjoyed the warm sun and the quiet breeze.

After they had traveled awhile, Bull slowed down.

Max said, "Let's find a comfortable place to rest. We need water." The three stopped and Max and Scooter jumped off Bull's back. While enjoying a drink they thought about the others they had left behind.

"With their lion speed and strength, Yoshi, Chai and Tiny will quickly turn Villa Zoo into a tidy home...wipe out all suspicions of wrongdoing! Morgan will have no clue of the day we've had," Scooter said.

Max looked up to the treetops. "I see signs of a thunderstorm. Some dark clouds are moving in and the wind is picking up," Max offered.

Bull took a moment to check his paws. They were in good condition. "Thanks to the toughness of this breed," thought Max.

"Let's get out of the mountains and home before the thunderstorm hits," said Scooter.

The MYSTC Lions climbed up onto Bull's back and they continued their descent to the bottom of the mountain...into the foothills and **FINALLY**, home.

After he had traveled a short distance, Bull stopped.

"What is it?" asked Max.

"I just saw the two black coyotes," said Bull.

"The black coyotes are rare," said Max. "We have to assume they are the same black coyotes that brought on all the chaos and caused harm to the mice and the pikas."

"And almost had us for their dinner," reminded Scooter.

"I've lost sight of them," said a concerned Bull.

Scooter turned his head, looking for some sign of the preying animals.

And came face to face with one of the coyotes.

Chapter Twelve

"Aaaah, Bull," Scooter said. "There's one behind us so don't back up." Bull slowly turned his head and saw the coyote. He immediately moved sideways looking for a safe spot to back up.

No one saw the second coyote. Bull continued to edge sideways while Scooter, keeping his eyes on the first coyote, took out the noisemaker. At the same time Scooter was removing the noisemaker, Bull began his ascent onto two legs. Max was hanging on and roaring...as loud as he could.

As Bull was turning on two legs to face the threatening coyote, Scooter lost his balance. He fell off Bull, striking the coyote. He ricocheted off the astonished coyote's head and bounced down a hill.

The noisemaker fell from his paws and hit the irate coyote...then bounced off the growling animal. The noise maker boomeranged off a stone and flew through the air, landing near a large rock at the bottom of a steep hill.

While Scooter was bumping and bouncing down the hill, Bull and Max realized both the noisemaker and Scooter were missing. The irritated coyote watched Scooter fall down the hillside, while keeping a threatening eye on Bull and Max. Not sure who he should hunt, he stood still but his eyes darted between the disappearing Scooter...and Max and Bull.

Bull stayed on his hind legs. He and Max made as much loud noise as they could raise while still looking frantically around for Scooter.

At the bottom of the hill, Scooter hit a rock...ending his momentum. Temporarily disoriented, he couldn't focus on his surroundings. When his head cleared, he saw the noisemaker laying next to him. While reaching for the noisemaker, he heard a low rolling growl. He turned around to face the menacing growl...and came eye-to-eye with the second coyote.

He remembered that Max and Bull were far away, at the top of the hill.

The coyote made his move towards Scooter. Keeping his eye on the stalking beast, Scooter used his large furry paw to reach the noisemaker. Once he touched the rattle, Scooter was up on his hind legs shaking the noisemaker wildly! He looked up and saw Bull and Max backing up on the hill above him. As one coyote stalked Bull and Max and the other coyote was inching toward Scooter, he knew he had to do something or they would be someone's meal.

Bull and Max were frantic, looking for Scooter and trying to keep away from the coyote.

All of a sudden, lightning cracked and the sky thundered. The coyote stalking Scooter suddenly turned and ran away in fear of the crackling noise.

Scooter watched the retreating coyote. When it disappeared behind a rock, he sped up the hill to find his friends. In leaps and bounds, Scooter reached the top of the steep hill and his buddies...just as the second coyote was about to take a bite out of Max's tail.

Lightning cracked and thunder shook the ground. Scooter waved the noisemaker with all his might. The coyote, frightened by the lightning cracks and thunder...and the noisemaker, took off after his partner.

Bull went down on all fours. He turned toward Scooter. He dug his paws into the earth and charged forward. He headed for home with Max hanging onto his reins. As they passed Scooter, he hopped onto Bull's back and held onto the pillow still attached around Bull's belly.

Bull ran as fast as his muscled legs would take him and his riders. They didn't slow down until Scooter, who was on watch for coyotes or bears or mountain lions, told Bull they had a clear path towards home.

"Scooter, are you okay?" asked Max. "You took quite a tumble."

"I'm fine," said Scooter. "A bump on my head...that's all."

Once the three heroes felt free of the danger, they moved at a slower pace down the mountain. Bull romped and the Lions bounced, laughing heartily. Max's glasses flew into the air and Scooter caught them.

"I'll hold onto these, chumbuddy, until we are in the house," Scooter said, then laughed.

All three of them were happy that their day had ended with everyone safe and a job well done.

"We managed to save everybody," Max said. "Thank you, Bull. Our trip up the mountain ended well. No one got hurt."

"I was worried about you, Scooter, when you fell and rolled out of sight," said Max.

"I'm a MYSTC Lion, Max. No worries," said a grinning Scooter. In the distance they saw the other Lions...Tiny, Yoshi and Chai...rushing to greet them.

"We cleared a path for your safe return," roared Yoshi. "Just in case you were in trouble, we wanted to offer our services."

"As a matter of fact," shy Chai said, "We just chased away two black coyotes with fire in their eyes. They were in the trees, watching."

"We were convinced they were waiting for you to reach the foothills and Villa Zoo. They didn't take kindly to the chase we put them through. With the thunder and lightning behind us and our roars and leaps, we made a pretty scary bunch of warriors," added a pumped up Yoshi.

"Where's Valentino?" asked Max.

"He said he was tired," answered Chai. "We left him curled up in his blankets but with one eye open, watching us and...waiting for Bull."

"We have stories to tell you when we get home," said Scooter. "Thanks for having our backs."

Soon their neighborhood was in sight. "Home," roared the MYSTC Lions. They laughed, elated with their day...everyone was safe.

The travelers entered Villa Zoo.

"We've had a successful journey," said Max as he jumped off Bull's back. He removed the pillows and reins and noisemaker and supplies. "Rocco and Hannah are home where they belong."

"We'll tell you all about it once we are settled downstairs," said Scooter. He followed Max off the big dog's back.

"I've had an eventful day, but I need to go home," said Bull. "Bitter G will be wondering where I am. Thank you for forgiving me for being a mean animal. I must have scared all of you...but you stood up to me!"

Max said, "Thank you for being our brave, helpful friend."

"Your knowledge of the Rockies saved us, Bull," Scooter added.

Valentino, waiting inside, saw his buddy Bull and ran over to him. It was a funny sight to see the two together, but the size difference didn't seem to bother them at all.

Valentino hopped up onto Bull's back and gave him a big hug. Bull ran around in a circle, careful not to make a shambles of the house this time. Valentino hopped off, and Bull was out the door and gone.

Max looked around. "I'm impressed with the order and calmness here. You all worked hard to clean up the mess we made. It's just what Morgan will expect when she arrives home."

The pantry doors were open but the food had been cleaned up. Nothing was out of place—except for the Tuna Power Cakes. They were on a shelf lower than the one Morgan had placed them on.

Max and Scooter looked at each other. Without saying a word, the two MYSTC Lions sprang into action.

Max, the more slender of the two, hopped up onto a ledge and crisscrossed the other shelves until he made it to the empty shelf. He stretched out his arms. His Lion buddy Scooter grabbed a package of cakes. Using his big paws, Scooter flipped the bag up to Max, who caught it and gently placed the bag on the proper shelf.

Stretching out his front paws again, Max grabbed the second bag on its way up. Once the Tuna Power Cakes were all placed on their rightful shelf, Max did a somersault into Scooter's waiting paws.

Then Scooter flipped Max over. He landed on his feet...his glasses still on his face. Max proudly held his head up...with a grin as big as his ego. Assuming an awesome swagger, Max left the pantry.

A grinning Scooter followed him, muttering, "Not bad for an old man."

Valentino, watching the gymnastics, shook his head. He turned and headed to his kennel, repeating over and over, "Dos gatos rudos."

"Valentino," said Yoshi, laughing, "you need a good rest with no interruptions. You've earned it."

The MYSTC Lions headed downstairs.

Before they could relax, the MYSTC Lions gathered in a circle on the floor. Each Lion, standing on his hind legs, paw patted the others. They roared, "United in Purpose...***No More!***"

The MYSTC Lions dropped to all fours. They watched as each other slowly mutated back... into the Cat Clan. The fierceness and fur peeled away leaving smiles, familiar faces and separate personalities. The strong muscled legs transformed into long and short, fat and skinny limbs. The giant hairy paws shrunk...replaced by delicate paws. Gone was the roar and the sharp teeth...replaced by playful meows and cat teeth. The magic and the Super Powers had gone away—for now.

Yoshi decided it had been awhile since he had chased Chai, and started off after her. As he began the chase, Chai screeched in fear. She took off, flying over a table and landing under the sofa... diaper and pearls intact.

Yoshi, tiring of the chase, decided to clean himself. He stretched his legs out in front of him... his white belly rippling to his tongue cleaning.

Chai was clearly tired. She went over by Yoshi and laid her weary head on his lap. When he was done licking his belly he licked Chai's tired head.

Yoshi, thinking a nap was a good idea, stretched out his body and laid his head down near Chai. Soon, they were both sound asleep, dreaming of Tuna Power Cakes.

A sleepy Tiny listened to Valentino snoring upstairs. Exhausted, Tiny climbed the stairs to be with her friend. Once there, she jumped onto the top of Valentino's kennel and lay down on the blanket she put there earlier. She curled up and fell asleep...squeaking every time Valentino snored.

A thirsty Scooter hopped up onto the counter. He turned on the faucet, and enjoyed a hefty drink. Refreshed, he leapt onto the sofa and up onto the ledge of the window to check the latch. He gazed outdoors...thinking about his day. Tonight, Scooter was content to stay in the house.

Max walked by and Scooter hissed at him. Max hissed back. "Hey. Don't bug me and stay out of my way," Max warned.

Giving Max a couple hisses and his backside, Scooter jumped to the sofa and fell into a deep slumber. He dreamt he was chasing mice...or were they chasing him?

Max looked around the room and hissed one more time at Scooter...for good measure. Then he saw the pillow he had been dreaming about that morning. "Was it just that morning?" he mused.

He grabbed the pillow with his teeth and dragged it to his water bowl. Once the pillow was half-submerged in water, he laid down on the other half and fell asleep. He dreamt about ruling the cat world.

Sometime later, the garage door opened and a car drove in. An exhausted family emerged from the SUV. Yawning while carrying blankets and bags into Villa Zoo, they crowded into the clean, quiet home...glad to be there.

Expecting a barking Valentino to greet them, there was only silence in the house.

In a tired voice Morgan said, "It is so good to come home to quiet and order after the busy day we've had. Our lucky animals got to relax and rest in a cool house all day." She laughed. "They'll probably be up all night."

Morgan eyed Bean and Wigs and grinned. "Apparently, someone left the downstairs door open." Morgan pointed to Tiny curled up on a blanket on the top of Valentino's kennel.

"Aunt Jillian told me during the tournament that she won't be home until tomorrow so we can lock the doors and settle in for the night," said Morgan.

"Mima is staying with friends. I'll call her and let her know all is well," said Morgan. "She was concerned. She'll sleep well knowing the animals had a quiet day."

"Since our rascally cats didn't get into trouble today, I think they've earned two Tuna Power Cakes tomorrow. I'll give each one of the cats two of the cakes for a treat instead of one. They can enjoy both...then take a long nap," said a generous but clueless Morgan.

Bean and Wigs ran downstairs to check on their pets.

Bean was amazed to see all of them resting. It appeared they were dreaming, with the biggest grins on their faces, as if they all shared the same secret.

Bean was surprised to see a long nail in the shape of a claw protruding from Chai's back paw as she rested her head on Yoshi.

"That's odd," she said. "Or...maybe not."

Bean realized that even though she didn't know what type of adventure they had that day, she knew they had one. She and Wigs shared a secret with them.

And she couldn't wait to tell Mima all about it.

The End... For Now!

TRANSMYSTC MUTATION
From a Meow to a ROAR!

Recite United In Purpose Oath

To Become Lions In Determination

EAT TWO TUNA POWER CAKES (TPCs) TO MUTATE

1. First TPC ~ Eat, Enjoy, Peace Flows
2. Second TPC ~ 1st bite within five minutes after 1st TPC

JOURNEY TO TRANSMYSTC MUTATION HAS BEGUN

Second TPC ~ continue eating until completed

AFTER MUTATION

Knead Brain Putty Until Lion Brains Reach Maximum Power

MAX   YOSHI   SCOOTER   TINY   CHAI

Note to Young Readers

Thank you for reading about Max, Scooter, Yoshi, Chai, Tiny, and their curious, mysterious happenings. They are so smart and brave. And that Valentino...he's an interesting chihuahua, full of love and mischief.

I love writing stories about animals for children to read and enjoy. If my wonderful bunch of heroic MYSTC Lions and their sidekick Valentino make you smile or even laugh out loud, then I have a happy heart. I believe, unconditionally, that children and animals are the innocents of our world and must be protected and cared for.

Mice don't belong in your home unless they've been invited in as your pet. But sometimes they wander in by mistake. So be gentle to a lost mouse. He's frightened and just wants to find his way back home.

You may never see a pika because they live so high up in the Rocky Mountains or in other places such as China, Eastern Europe, as well as Asia and North America. Pikas love cold weather. They are adorable, aren't they? They have a good work ethic and are gentle souls. The pika looks like a little rabbit and is sometimes called a Rock Hare. The pika's squeak sounds like a mouse.

And best of all, Pikachu, a favorite Pokémon, is said to be inspired by the pika. Some discussions say Pikachu is a squirrel, but the pika in this book looks and sounds similar to Pikachu. You can read about the pika and discover all about it in the library.

Happy learning dear children, and thank you for reading *The Curious Mysterious Happenings of Valentino and the MYSTC Lions*.

About the Author

J.J. Kat wrote poetry as a young girl and well into adulthood.

As that young girl in the Midwest, she had a favorite spot near streaming water flowing playfully over large rocks. On warm, sunny days, with a forest of trees as a backdrop, she would sit on a small hill of large white stone slabs near the stream. The silence freed the poetic words from her thoughts and she would write them down as they spilled from her heart and her mind. Only in peace would these words find her notebook.

As years passed and she grew to the age of a college student, she frequently went seeking that same solitude...that only nature's water and trees could provide.

When she was twenty-one and headed to New York City on a rolling train, watching the world rush by, she knew she wanted to write a book.

After New York City and many years in Chicago, she followed her life's journey to Denver, Colorado. She fell in love with Colorado...where she lived for many years. J.J. Kat found serenity in the small towns in the Rocky Mountains outside of Denver. The dancing Aspen trees, cool mountain nights and warm sunny days forged a memory so vivid that years later she could still remember the harmony and delight the soul experienced from being a part of that beauty.

Climbing the mountains on foot or horseback leaves an experience never to be duplicated for the challenge and endurance it encourages. With an urgency to move forward by the breezy trees and the sheer will of accomplishment, she reached many a mountain top.

So it just seemed fitting that her animals from her first book should be a part of the beautiful experience of the Colorado Rockies.

She fell in love with a Colorado native and had her two daughters.

It wasn't until many years later that a move to De Pere, Wisconsin and the births of her grandchildren that she realized that long ago dream of writing a book. Because of her love for the innocents of the world... children and animals...it was natural that she wrote about them in the first book of her three book series.

Visit JJKatAuthor.com or Facebook.com/JJKatAuthor
to learn more about J.J. Kat and her book series.

The Curious Mysterious Happenings of Valentino and the MYSTC Lions

Acknowledgments

Thank you to **Mary Grace Murphy**, friend and fellow author, for her honest and appreciated comments. She not only read through the first draft but offered good and helpful comments as she read through the final daft. You've been a good friend, and I thank you for all your support as I introduce Valentino and the MYSTC Lions to children everywhere.

In the literary world, Mary Grace is best known for her cozy mysteries:

DEATH NELL • DEATH NOSH • DEATH KNOCK

Thank you to my good friend **Trisha** and her sister **Sarah** for reading my final draft and offering their very constructive opinions about my story of five funny and wonderful cats and their friend Valentino.

Thank you to **Yolanda Hernandez** for her unending support both emotional and technical. Her illustrations and graphic knowledge helped us get this book published.

Yolanda and I do readings together. I read and she creates some incredible sound effects to bring the story alive and keep the young listeners on the edge of their seats. Our readings are known as "Sounds Amid The Tale."

Thank you to Illustrator **Austin Decker**, 15 years old, for creating some wonderful illustrations.

Thank you to my beautiful granddaughter, **Ella Lauren**, for all the nights she wanted me to read to her before she slept. You are special and, I know, will grow into a wonderful, kind adult.

Continued...

Acknowledgments ~ Continued

Thank you to my wonderful grandson, *Cameron*, age 10, for his endearing contribution to my first book…"the paper flying over the rooftop" illustration. When you are a grown man with children of your own, you can be proud to show your children how much you supported and believed in your Mima. Thank you my handsome, smart grandson for believing in me.

When Yolanda and I did a reading at Cam's school to his, at that time, nine year old class, he took charge of the reading. He introduced me and stayed vital throughout the reading.

A special thank you to *Mark Shamlian* for creating the character illustrations on the front and back covers of my first book. Yolanda added the mice and the sweet pikas to the back cover.

Thank you to my good friend *Bonnie* and my sister *Linda* for believing in me.

On a bitterly cold day for my first reading, a September outdoor children's party, there was my family wrapped in blankets clapping and smiling. Thank you *Kate* and *Jill*, *Ella* and *Cam*, *Kevin* and *Charles* for supporting and loving me.

Thank you to Stella's in De Pere Wisconsin…and to *Mike Oldenburg* and *Shawn Zambarda* for all your hospitality. Yolanda and I spent many nights at the "Table In The Corner" editing my first children's book.

Thank You!

English Glossary

Astute .... of keen penetration or discernment

Burrowed .... a hole or tunnel in the ground

Canny .... careful, cautious, prudent
Colossal .... extraordinarily great in size
Commence .... to begin, start
Convulse .... to shake violently

Elevation .... the height to which something rises
Embedded .... to settle into a surrounding mass
Encircled .... to form a circle around
Entangled .... to make tangled. Intertwine.
Extricate .... to free or release from entanglement

Gnawing .... biting or chewing on persistently
Guffawed .... a loud, unrestrained burst of laughter

Illuminate .... to supply or brighten with light; light up
Insightful .... perceptive; show keenness of understanding

Mantra .... words chanted as a prayer or vision
Mystifying .... to bewilder, to perplex

Nonchalantly ...... coolly unconcerned, indifferent or unexcited

Orator .... a public speaker, a person with great eloquence

Pandemonium .... wild uproar. Tumult or chaos
Pilfering .... to steal in small quantities
Pitiful .... deserving pity
Propelled .... to cause to move forward or onward

Quaking .... shake or tremble from fear or anger or cold

Scuffling .... to struggle or fight in a rough manner
Scurry .... to move quickly or in haste
Shuttered .... to close

Treeline .... the altitude above sea level at which timber ceases to grow
Turmoil .... a state of great commotion, confusion

Wary .... watchful, being on guard
Wavered .... to feel or show doubt. To shake or tremble
Within .... in or into the interior or inner part
Woodlands .... land covered with woods or trees

Spanish Glossary

Ay .... Oh

Ay caramba .... Oh No

Ay chihuahua .... Expression of dismay, annoyance

Ayudame .... Help me

Dos Gatos Rudos .... Two Rude Cats

Mira Mira .... Look Look

No me siento bien .... I do not feel well

No puedo creer que .... I can't believe I slept with
me haya acostado con   them in the same space
ellos en el mismo espacio

Patada .... Kick

Enjoy this Excerpt from Book II:
The Curious Mysterious Happenings On The Zion Express

The knock on the door of Villa Zoo was hushed by barking from a bouncing chihuahua wearing a white collar etched with red kisses.

Mima thought she heard the door chime. Alarmed by sudden pounding, she cautiously walked to the white-panelled entry. She listened...and slowly opened the heavy door.

"Just a peek," she thought. "Someone may be in trouble."

She looked through the small opening of the door...and **GASPED IN HORROR!**

"Max", said Scooter, roused from a nap in the sunshine by the irritating noises coming from upstairs, "There's so much barking coming from that runt of a watch dog...let's send him to another planet."

The others from the Cat Clan stirred, raised their sleepy heads and meowed. After some stretching, the tired felines settled back into the warmth of the sun.

"Scooter", said a concerned Max. "Mima's upstairs, alone! I'm worried she's in trouble. I need to get to her quickly."

A giant animal charged into Villa Zoo through the small opening of the door Mima held open. The creature knocked her on his way into the large home...causing her to lose her balance. The door swung wide...pulling Mima with it.

A chill encircled the hot mountain air and followed the huge beast into Mima's home. Regaining her balance, she shuddered from the cold.

Gripped with fear, she couldn't take her eyes off the looming spook standing over her.

"Why is this monster here? He's gone mad," she thought. "Now his beast is inside Villa Zoo and this madman is at my door...trying to get inside."

Panicked, Mima tried to shut the entry...but it wouldn't close. Something or someone was blocking the large door. All she wanted to do was grab her family and run for safety inside Villa Zoo.

"It's Bitter GasBritches and he's finally come to hurt us!" she cried.

CPSIA information can be obtained
at www.ICGtesting.com
Printed in the USA
LVHW021527050121
675633LV00013B/343